LOST IN
AMBITION

Steve Pederson

ISBN: 1543184847
ISBN 13: 9781543184846

For Tami

TABLE OF CONTENTS

CHAPTER 1

LOCKER ROOM

I n about thirty minutes, I am coaching in the College Football National Championship game and trying to figure out why I am not more excited.

I have literally sacrificed everything to get here, and this is how I feel? I can't explain it. This is supposed to be the dream. A small-town kid rises to head coach at a big-time university and now has a chance to play for it all. It is probably the dream of many young kids. I think it was mine, but right now I can't remember.

All I can think about is what I am going to say after the game today, win or lose. This is really hard, and it's not supposed to be that way.

"Coach, the specialists are on the field. Are you ready to go?" Cal Smith is our Director of Football Operations. He is a good guy. He's pretty efficient, the players like him, and he knows how to keep his mouth shut. That might be his greatest trait. I really rely on him and he could bury me if he wanted to. I didn't intend for him to get in the middle of so much. Heck, I didn't plan to get in the middle of so much stuff. It just kind of happened, which is not necessarily a good thing.

"Coach, are you okay?" Cal asks in kind of a panic. "I'm fine Cal, let's go get 'em," I say.

With that, I'm off to coach the game of a lifetime. As I walk out of the coaches' locker room, it hits me like a blast of cold air. Is this really what I wanted? I can't get the conversation with my dad out of my head.

You see, I grew up pretty simply, in a small town in Ohio where my dad was the Principal and the Head Football Coach. (In Ohio, it seems to me the coaching job is a lot more prestigious.) When I do interviews now, everyone wants to know if I grew up dreaming about coaching like my dad. I give them a good answer, but the reality is when you are in your teens, you seldom grow up dreaming about anything other than having fun and enjoying your friends.

Do you want to have a great life? Of course, you do. But to think that at a young age you were focused on your career, I don't think so. But things happen and you're really not in control anymore. That's what happened to me. I woke up one day and everything was different. I'm not sure when I lost control of all of this, but I really can't seem to slow it down.

I was a good kid, never a problem for my folks and I would say that most of the other parents wanted their sons around me. Dad was the Principal, we went to church every Sunday, and Mom was nice, sweet, and welcoming. I had two little sisters who worshiped me. Sounds like a simple life. It really was as simple as it sounds. I remember being happy every day and I sure don't remember ever being bored. I grew up in a town of 5,000 people and I don't remember being restless for one minute.

Maybe when you have too much, you can't figure out what to do next or something. I hear it all the time from our current players. Like, I am supposed to entertain them or something?

As I think about where I am today, there was one specific day that sticks out in my mind. It was the day the legendary Ohio State Football Coach, Woody Hayes, came to town to visit my dad's school. It was like the President of the United States had arrived. The entire town was electric because Coach Hayes was coming. I got to meet him and shake his hand. I was only 6 years old, but I remember thinking how cool it must be to be the coach that everyone revered. Now I am that guy.

I was a pretty good player in high school, not an Ohio State or Michigan kind of player, but had a lot of interest from MAC schools and others. For some reason, I just wanted to do something different, so I headed south to play at Eldridge College. Everyone told me it was a great school and I would get a good job after I graduated. My sisters were devastated. How could I go so far away from them? I'm not sure they knew where North Carolina was, much less the town of Eldridge. It's a beautiful place nestled in the heart of the mountains, a private school with an enrollment of around 6,000. It was the right size for me.

I knew going to a college so far away was selfish. With Dad coaching high school football, he was never going to get to one of my games anyway. I did feel bad that Mom and the girls were so far away, but it was what seemed right at the time. Maybe that should have been an indication to me that I was a selfish guy. I just knew I wanted to do this and did it, regardless of whether it hurt other people. You know, you can't be so worried about what other people think. You do what is right for you.

If there is one thing I know from watching successful coaches, they don't give a damn about what is in their way. They just go for it. Look at many of the great ones in history. They make the rules fit them and when they win, the fans stick right by them (of course, as long as they keep winning). It's the rules of the game and only lightweights don't understand that. You see, if you want to play for the big prize, you have to cut a few corners, but that's a little secret and we don't need to make a big deal about that.

"Hey Cal," I say as we walk to the field. "I assume we got everyone seated appropriately?" "Yes, sir. Cyndy and the kids are at the

50-yard line behind our bench with the other coaches' wives and families. Julia is on the 50 on the opposite sideline. I have seat numbers so you can pick them out."

I can't believe that my team is playing for the National Championship and the President of the university takes the luxury suite, leaving my family sitting in the stands. What a prick! Of course, what am I going to do with a suite? Wife or girlfriend? Saves me a hell of a decision!

"Thanks, Cal. You always get things handled. I won't forget that." Hell, no I won't forget, and he knows I can't afford not to remember. Oh yeah, some fans would forgive me for these indiscretions, but others would think less of me. Much of that will depend on my coaching record!

Forget those thoughts, time to think about a postgame photo on the field with Cyndy and the kids. Let's hope it's a victory photo.

CHAPTER 2
GETTING STARTED

As I walk to the field, the juices start to flow. The crowd roars at every little thing that happens. The punter is warming up, and with each kick, the fans cheer like it is a live game. Of course, they have probably been drinking since mid-morning and now they are fired up about everything. Some fans may not even make it to the end of the game.

I have never figured that out. Why would you get so drunk before a big game that you either pass out or miss the entire game? I will bet most of these people paid scalpers for tickets, maybe $2,000 each or higher. How can you miss the game?

Here is a funny little secret about these kinds of games. I get an extra 20 tickets to this game as part of my contract. I am supposed to use them for family and friends, but the friends can buy their own tickets. This is another one of Cal's jobs. He sells my 20 tickets for the highest price he can get, and makes certain no one knows they are my tickets. The only requirement is they have to be our fans. I can't have a bunch of asshole fans from the opposing team in our section creating problems.

But let's be real, I can get $2,500 a ticket for these seats. That's $50,000. I have to pay for Julia's apartment and trips somehow. I used to take the money from the summer football camp, but the university auditors look at that stuff, so it is more complicated. You have to be creative and you have to have some good friends, like my car dealer. He's a great guy and gets it, if you know what I mean. He is the only person I could ask to give a car to my girlfriend and trust that it remains confidential. We are drinking buddies, so it was easier to ask. That, and the fact that he has three women driving his cars and only one of them is his wife! He runs in the fast lane and he's just what I need. Oh, don't worry, I take good care of him also. It's a true friendship.

Now before you think I am a total jerk, I do take care of my family with game tickets. My parents, my sisters and their families, Cyndy's parents and her brother. I just have to lie a little. I went to see the athletic director and made up some story about not realizing the 20 tickets were for my family and I need more. He probably knows I am lying my ass off, but what is he going to do? The fans love me and the President, his boss, is a total candy ass who just wants to be in every photo with me. The athletic director doesn't really have a choice but to give me the tickets, right? Besides, he gets a bonus if I win, so he's not stupid.

He is also aware that my agent is already starting to float my name out there for other jobs, including pro jobs. Nothing is specific yet, but it starts the bees buzzing around the hive. Our big donors' egos won't allow another team to buy me away. We have gone through this dance each of the last two years and that is how I went from $2 million to $4 million a year in salary. They give me a new contract, lots of money, and then I stand up and say it is all about loyalty to the program. The great part is they all eat it up, and think I am sincere. It's all part of the deal, so I play right along.

As I hit the field I see Carl Samuels, our wide receivers coach. He reminds me of myself at a younger age. I brought him with me the day I got this job. He is so wound up he can hardly contain himself. He's young, single, and coaching on a team playing for the National Championship where he has recruited many of our best players. He gets it and is willing to do whatever it takes to recruit them. I don't know when you get that way, but one day, even good guys turn.

When I was his age, I started out convinced I could do this the right way. I didn't like the cheaters, and told myself I could do it without cheating. Then reality hits and you are trying to recruit guys. Your salary depends on it, your next job depends on it, and maybe, most importantly, your ego depends on it. In our business, we all know the guys who get it done.

It's funny though, the NCAA never seems to figure that out. Maybe they don't really want to. College sports is big business. The head of the NCAA makes several million dollars a year and he's not going overboard to bring order. Every once in a while, the NCAA will try and find someone to nail, but it's usually not the "big boys." There is too much at stake.

Sometimes I look at Carl and think, if I were really a good guy, I would talk to him and tell him to get the hell out of this business before he is too far gone. He is smart and he can make it doing something else. But he probably can't make several million dollars a year unless he is a head coach. That's the key, the money changes everything. It changed me.

I think back to my first job as a graduate assistant at Kentucky College. They paid for my schooling so I could get a Master's Degree. Honestly, why in the hell does a coach need a master's degree? I think it's just a way to pay young guys poorly, and justify the salary. It was, actually, a great time in my life. I loved the little things. The free meals at the training table, the head coach asking you to drive him to a speaking engagement (time with the head coach was considered gold). I didn't really have any money, but I didn't really need any. All I did was work, so I couldn't do anything anyway. It was simple and it was exciting.

One day our head coach, Bob Dudley, came down the hall to see me. He said, "I just recommended you for the running backs job at Birmingham State. It's a great opportunity in a state where the three most important things are college football, college football and college football." I was ecstatic, not just because it was a full-time job, but because it was in Alabama, where the football coach was the most admired man in the state. Now, I just couldn't blow the interview.

I knew I had a good chance at the job because my current head coach was well respected and an endorsement from him was a big plus. I also knew the coach at Birmingham State was tough. He was a little bandy rooster kind of guy, the son of a legendary college football coach, and he had won a lot of games. I didn't have enough experience for him to be impressed with me. I had to be knowledgeable and appear both mature and tough. He liked tough.

The interview was worse than I thought. First of all, these are not rich schools, so they told me to drive myself to Birmingham and they would have a hotel room for me. The first night's dinner was with two coaches, the offensive coordinator and the quarterbacks coach. It seemed like they were best friends. As it turned out, they were. The quarterback coach, Daniel Quick, was the brains and the offensive coordinator, Hartley King, was the offensive line coach and probably of average intelligence. The dinner that night seemed to be nothing about football. I think they just wanted to see if they liked me. I was trying my best to fit in, but the drunker Coach King got, the harder it became. Coach Quick tried to keep things on track, but King seemed angry. I said, "what's it like to work for Coach Jackson?" His response, "He's a prick and you'll go home most nights, when you finally get to go home, hating his guts. He is a complete asshole." Quick tried to soften things by saying, "you have probably heard that Coach is tough, but he will make you the best coach you have ever been. Isn't that what you want?"

Heck yes, that is what I want. I want to coach at the big time and, to do that, I better be at the top of my game. In some ways, I now felt at ease knowing how to handle the meeting with Coach Jackson. If you are going to be good at something, you had better get over hurt feelings, and understand that toughness is about the most important quality in football. If I can stomach a few more hours of this drunk, I'll be ready for the interview in the morning.

CHAPTER 3
THE INTERVIEW

If I could trace the trajectory of my career to any one thing, it would be the interview with Coach Jackson. No matter how ready or confident I thought I was, nothing could have prepared me for this moment.

In high school, my dad was a good coach. He did pretty well most years and won the league title a few times. I think kids liked playing for him and he had reasonable expectations. That being said, he was not one to push to extremes, but then high school coaches should probably not do that anyway. The ones who do usually wind up with a bunch of kids who hate football.

My coach at Eldridge College, Bill Starr, was a really nice man, what they like to call a "players' coach." I was never really sure what that meant except he was probably too easy on us. Now, any time I hear someone referred to as a players' coach, I think to myself, "he must be a loser who wants all the players to like him, so he never really demands much from them." This type of coach never really does anything big, but he generally wins enough games to keep his job. The players see to that.

I liked playing football in college and got to play a lot. I was the starting quarterback for three years. We had reasonable success winning nine games each of my three starting seasons. But nine wins gives you just enough ammunition to talk about how close you were to winning them all. For the coach, it is justification of progress to the administration, and keeps fans focused on what might happen next year. Woody Hayes used to say, you are either getting better or you are getting worse, you never stay the same. I could make the argument that a lot of coaches keep their jobs by staying the same. Woody Hayes, of course, was no players' coach.

Everyone at Eldridge loved Coach Starr. He walked across campus every day to eat at the Faculty Club. He loved to hold court there, telling stories about the last game, or the time he coached against Bear Bryant, or give predictions on who was going to win the big game. He was smart and he knew almost all the faculty and the administration. Remember, Eldridge College is a small private school in a small town. He was always careful to make sure everyone knew that academics came first in his program. He was sincere about that, too. He recruited good kids and didn't play the ones who weren't going to class or were flunking out. The faculty loves that kind of commitment, and it's easier at a small school. No one expects you to be playing in the championship game.

If you want to win a title, you better get guys who can play football and forget about the academic part. Besides, we pay our tutors and counselors well to make sure the players stay eligible. Ultimately that is our goal. Oh yeah, we talk about graduation and that always sounds good in public settings. We say this to our team, but the players are about as serious as the coaches are about it. They want to get to the NFL and they don't need a degree for that.

I know I sound cynical, but I'm really not. It is the reality of all this, and the ones who forget about that are out of a job pretty quickly. I heard the coach at Capital State quoted as saying that except for a few walk-ons, no one on his team could get into Capital State on his own. That was probably not popular on campus, but they are no different than any other school.

Even when I was playing in college, I had the strong feeling that we should expect more. You should not win nine games and celebrate. However, I was in the minority on my team. The rest seemed to love "just being good enough." That's okay, but it hung onto me like a vine, not letting me go. This can be better, I can be better, and I have got to get to a place with people more like me. That is sometimes easier said than done.

That's how I got to Kentucky College. I knew I needed to start as a graduate assistant at a place where they won. They were coming off four consecutive conference titles and were the best team in their league by far. I knew the coach was well regarded and being mentored by him was a good thing for me, either there, or if he got a bigger job. See, you always have to attach yourself to those who are going places. Coaches move, that's what they do. Better school, better pay, better title. They never plan to stay anywhere very long. It's a tough life, particularly on families. You just seem to get settled, and then it is time to move again. Right then that didn't concern me. I was young, single, and ready to go anywhere I needed to go for a good job. I was only responsible for myself and that's a great feeling. And, by the way, the girls love coaches, especially the young ones full of energy and excitement. There are some freaks out there, but if you are close to the players, they will warn you about the ones to stay away from as a coach or player.

Kentucky College was exactly what I had hoped. It enjoyed a winning culture and the coach was a demanding guy, but also fair. It made me realize right away that this was exactly what I wanted.

There were just two graduate assistants. The other guy was the son of a famous NFL coach who was known as an outspoken, tough guy who couldn't get along with anybody. The son, however, was a really good guy, just dirt lazy. Clearly, his dad had gotten him the job and the head coach figured this favor would pay dividends for him in the future. The problem for me was that it meant I had to do everything. It was like Bob got a free pass because of his last name.

This was just my first taste of the politics of college football. I told myself no sense complaining, just get to work. What I didn't know was that all the coaches knew exactly what was going on. That is how, after only two years, I got this interview at Birmingham State. In the minds of the coaching staff, I had earned it.

"You're a GA, you haven't recruited, you haven't really done shit, so why in the hell would I ever hire you?" No introduction, no hand-shake. Those were the first words out of the mouth of Coach Jackson, as he stood in the doorway of his office, loud enough that everyone within 100 yards could hear. "If I didn't like Coach Dudley so much, you wouldn't even be here wasting my time." Coach King had warned me, but this guy was a Grade A asshole. I have two choices now, fold my tent and run for the door, or fight it out and see if I can win him over. I have a theory about a guy like this. Most of what you see is an act, meant to grow his persona to gigantic proportions. People will stand around and tell stories about just how bad it is to work for him. It seems like the boosters in particular love these kinds of stories, the kind that make him seem like an extraordinary person. "He takes shit from no one." They say this with complete admiration.

It is funny. No booster or alum would ever work for a guy like that, but they love hearing the stories about how someone else had to endure it.

"Let's get this over with," says Coach Jackson, waving me into his office. There is something about a head coach's office that is generally designed to be intimidating. It can be a good kind of in-timidation, like when you are trying to impress a five-star player or trying to keep a current player from going home. But just the op-posite for a player in trouble or a young GA interviewing for a job. He settles in behind the big desk, too big for a guy who coaches football, and I sit in a chair in front, which seems designed particu-larly low so he is peering down on me.

"What makes you think you can coach running backs here suc-cessfully?" I had been prepared for a question like this so I gave him my answer, pretty much the stuff you might expect. His response, "I'm not impressed. I think this is a waste of my time." I am furious, he hasn't even said my name, if he even knows it, and is not giving me a fair shot. Again, I have two choices. I can get up and leave or take a big chance. What the heck, it couldn't really get worse from here.

"You haven't spent five minutes with me or asked me anything of substance. Now you are telling me I am wasting your time. Here is what I am going to do. I am going to leave here, get a job at another school in this league, and make it my mission to kick your ass in recruiting and on the field every single year. How's that for wasting your time?" With that, I get up and head for the door.

CHAPTER 4
PUT UP OR SHUT UP

High risk can often mean high reward. My arrogant retort to Coach Jackson was exactly what he was hoping to hear. Are you tough enough, competitive enough, and do you want it bad enough? Two days later I was driving back to Birmingham with all my belongings in the car. I was starting my first full time job as an assistant football coach at Birmingham State.

I felt great walking into the football offices for the first time. It was like this was meant to be, and I was exactly where I belonged. I had made some pretty bold statements about what I was capable of doing. Now I was at the point, as my grandfather used to say, to either put up or shut up, and I was working for a guy who believed that times ten! Here's the reality. They hired me to recruit players. The coaching part was secondary. The great coaches know if you have nine assistants, about four must be able to coach and the other five better recruit great players. So, while I need to be at my best as a coach, my survival depends on recruiting success. Some assistants never get this. They sit in the film room and become geniuses of the X's and O's. They become coordinators on offense or defense and build a good reputation as a coach. Unfortunately, most are failures as head coaches because they never get the recruiting part. By the same token, some pretty average football coaches have won a lot of games because they had better players than the other team. Having better players accounts for about 80% of the victories in college football. Don't believe otherwise.

While I was prepared to go to work, I wasn't quite prepared for the reality of recruiting success. Jimmy Dykes, our recruiting coordinator, is an upbeat guy and seems ready to help me succeed. Of course, if I succeed, he looks good as well and we all win.

"Let's go get a beer," Jimmy says about 2 p.m. on Wednesday. We head to some dive bar near the campus. It is the middle of the week so it is nearly empty. "So, how much did Coach fill you in?" he asks me in kind of a sneaky manner. "About what in particular?" I ask. Jimmy says, "about getting players here. You don't think they are coming here because they like the business school, do you? This is a good place, we win a lot, football is important here, but the schools we recruit against aren't going to play fair, so we can't afford to either." I am silent.

"I am going to introduce you to a man named Gary Waters. He's the President of the biggest bank in town and our best booster. He is a Birmingham State graduate and will do anything he can for us. We like to keep this all tight, so Gary is the only guy you should talk to about this stuff. He is magic. Keep him connected and magically recruits will appear before you," he chuckles.

"Don't you worry about getting caught?" I ask. He laughs, "who is going to turn you in? Whatever we are doing, others are doing exactly the same. It's the way it is down here. Plus, that's why Gary is so great. You never have to do anything yourself and Coach Jackson is completely insulated. It's a pretty good system but you have to be smart about how you use it."

I felt like I had been punched in the stomach. I guess I knew at some level that there was a lot of cheating going on. But I just didn't realize it was so organized, matter of fact, and that I was going knee deep into it. Sometimes I feel so stupid, like it's all supposed to be like you see in television features about how players chose one school over another. I think long and hard, because once you cross that line, you can never go back. My parents raised me to do the right thing, but they can't possibly understand big time college football. I have a decision to make, I either go for it, or give up on my dream. I'll be damned if I will give up on this dream.

The reality is cheating does pay dividends. How many times have you seen a school that has struggled for years, win big with a new coach? Great coaching, I don't think so. Great players, yes. And how do they get them? You can usually watch the pattern. The coach wins and then leaves for a bigger job. Soon the school goes right back to mediocre. Here's the best part. No one talks because they are all in on it. Coaches won't talk, players won't talk, boosters won't talk. There are too many bad implications for everyone involved. The biggest risk is a player finds out what you are doing for his teammate. That doesn't go over well and you need to be ready to deal with a jealous player.

So, I am three days into the job, and my first step across the line is imminent. Oh well, I rationalize that everyone else is doing it so it must be okay. Still, there is a sinking feeling as I realize that this literally changes everything, and I am changed forever.

On Saturday, we are all invited to a barbecue at Gary Waters' house. I guess this is pretty standard stuff. You buy access when you get this involved. This isn't an optional event either. You are expected to attend and act very appreciative.

Gary Waters is a short man, maybe 5'8', but weighs about 250 pounds. He is the kind of red-faced guy who looks like he is going to burst at any time. His wife, Gail, is a nice-looking woman in her mid-50's, I would guess. It is hard to tell exactly how old, because she has had so much work done. I guess that is what you do when the kids are out of the house and you have a lot of money. Seems weird to me though. There wasn't much of that in Ohio, at least not that I knew about.

"Well here's the new guy. Welcome to Birmingham State, son. I hear you are a pistol, which is good. Coach needs another one of those on his staff. Seems like recruiting has been a little weak the past couple of years and we can't have that, now can we?" Gary Waters says as he puts his arm around me. "Meet Gail, she's the real football fan in the family." I can see this is the standard line and Gail probably tired of it about ten years ago, but she smiles and goes along. What some people will do for a $3 million house, a Mercedes, and an unlimited budget. "Make yourself at home. I see you are alone. You need to meet our daughter, Cyndy. She doesn't really want to be here either so you two can keep each other company," Gail says.

Panic sets in. I need these people to make it here, and now I am getting set up with their daughter. I am imagining a female version of Gary.

"This is Cyndy," Gail exclaims. If there is ever a time in your life where you are completely at a loss for words, you understand exactly how I feel at this moment. In front of me is the most beautiful girl I have ever seen in my life. It's like I am a third party to all of this. I can't get any words to come out. Finally, I manage a "pleased to meet you". She is laughing now, "I know, my mom says, come meet my daughter and you are thinking, oh no". Not only is she beautiful, but she has a sense of humor. "This was pre-planned you know. I wouldn't be here except they insisted and showed me a picture of you," she says laughing. "My dad has always wanted me to date a coach. How's that for low expectations?" she says with a twinkle in her eye.

"What makes you think I want to date you?" I say getting my wits about me again. "I like that. I don't know if it is confidence or arrogance, but it sells. Do you want a drink? My dad has everything," Cyndy says.

So here I am, one week into the job and crazy about our top booster's daughter. Sounds like a disaster waiting to happen.

Ninety-nine times out of one hundred, that would be the case. The difference here is Cyndy, who just makes everything right. I have already figured out that the coach who makes it to the top has a great wife to support what he does. She has to be able to make players, recruits, and boosters comfortable, and she has to be willing to accept a life where her husband is never home. Sounds appealing, huh? But there is a level of excitement that draws women in.

Maybe it is because she grew up watching her parents and their admiration for coaches, but I sense early on that Cyndy craves and understands this kind of exciting lifestyle. Best of all, she seems to like me. This all seems to be spinning very fast, but I am certainly the better for it.

CHAPTER 5

REALITY

The first real taste of working for Coach Jackson comes the opening day of spring practice. Historically, the first day of spring practice is generally not a great practice. The players have just come off spring break, where they did as little as possible. The seniors are gone, so you have a lot of new guys in important positions. It has been several months since we practiced together, so the rhythm is not good. As a coach, you understand this. You expect it to a large extent, but it still infuriates you. Three hours on the field in semi-confusion is perfect fodder for the head coach to snap. I've seen this before, where a tirade sets the tone for the rest of the spring. However, I have never witnessed anything like I am about to hear.

Whistles are blowing all over the place with the bull horn calling everyone together in the middle of the field. It seems like there is shouting and yelling by everyone wearing a coaching shirt. To an outsider, this must look like a comedy. To those on the inside, it is perfectly natural and justified. "Everybody up," shouts the football operation director Doug Johnson. "All eyes on Coach."

Coach Jackson stands silent for a minute, making it very awkward. Then he very slowly says, "I want to apologize to you fellas.

This is my fault, not yours. If I had hired better coaches, practice wouldn't look like this. This sorry ass bunch of coaches couldn't get you ready to beat a good high school team. Don't worry, I'll get rid of every damn one of them and get you some real coaches in here. You deserve better coaching and you're not getting it. Let's get this practice over with and get inside."

We are fifty minutes into a three-hour practice. I am thinking, great, I just get here and he tells the players that I can't coach, and the staff is getting fired. He puts none of this on the players, no accountability. I cannot figure this out. How does he think this makes us a better team?

When the whistle blows and practice resumes, I am somewhat in a daze. Coach Quick runs by me and slaps me on the back. "Watch this," he says. All of a sudden, practice comes to life, as if a completely different football team is on the field. The energy is high, execution becomes crisp, and the players are responding to coaching in a completely different manner. All of the sudden my players are fixated on everything I say. We finish practice and everyone heads to the locker room.

I am still trying to figure out what happened. As I walk off the field, Tom Connor, our trainer, joins me. "The guy is pretty good, isn't he?" Tom says. "Tom, what in the hell just happened out there?" I ask. "Let's go in my office and sit down," he says with a warm smile.

Trainers are always so important to a team. For medical reasons, obviously, but that is really about 50% of their job. They are psychologists, best friends, confidants, advisors, just about everything to the players. At least the good trainers are and Tom is one of the best. He seems to have his pulse on everything.

Trainers are generally overworked and underpaid. They are in many ways underappreciated but not by the players. Players and trainers enjoy a special bond.

As we sit down in his cramped office, one of our players pokes his head in the door. "Thanks for calling my mom last night. She feels a lot better now," he says. Tom responds, "No problem. She just worries about you and I do, too." After the player leaves, Tom says, "girlfriend problems and the mom is worried he is going to do something stupid. I think he is more worried about his mom's response than the girl." Another problem solved in the training room.

"You will eventually see why he wins like he does," referring to Coach Jackson. "He has a magical way of pulling all the pieces together to build team culture. That little stunt out there is typical. I saw him do that about five years ago. If he calls all the players together and yells at them, cusses a blue streak, and tells them they are worthless, they get mad, particularly at him. Practice doesn't really get any better. Our players like these coaches. Currently, you are the only coach they are trying to figure out, because you are new. If new coaches come in, the players worry they might drop down the depth chart, or that the offensive system will change. Players really care mostly about themselves. The less change, the easier it is for them. So, what Coach just did was put you all in this together. He's on one side, the coaches and players on the other. The only way you survive is to make each other look good. Did you see how the players responded?"

I said, "it was actually amazing to watch. I just got a lesson in psychology of football and the creation of team dynamics." "If you really pay attention, you can build your own portfolio of ideas to use down the line," Tom responds.

"Thanks, Tom. I have a lot to learn around here." He says, "I've been here eight years and I still do also." We both laugh, shake hands, and get back to business.

As I head back to the coaches' locker room to change, Carlos Johnson, our star tailback, stops me in the hallway. "Don't worry when Coach gets like that. We've got your back," he tells me. "He gets like that sometimes, but he's alright." So now I am starting to see the entire program in a different light. It is interesting to be a part of this. Everyone knows his role and what it takes to succeed. Without prompting, a 21-year old kid knows how to build a relationship with a new assistant coach. Culture is a powerful ingredient, maybe the most important of all.

"Thanks, Carlos. You guys were terrific today after Coach got mad. I'm glad I am here and appreciate you fellas helping the new guy out."

Here is another thing I do know. The key to recruiting is what your players say about the program. As a coach, you do everything possible to close the deal, but a player will never lie to another player, so being close to your team is very important. When the recruits are on their official visits to campus, away from the coaching staff, what the current players say is the most important factor of all. I am going to need these guys on and off the field if I want to be successful.

As I head into the locker room, the rest of the assistants are showered and dressed, and sitting on stools in front of their lockers talking. "We thought maybe you quit already," says Milt Tingle, our tight ends coach. They all laugh. "I wasn't ready for that, but it was amazing to watch. You have got to love our players," I said. "Yes, they probably understand him better than we do," says Milt.

After a shower, I begin what is to become pretty much the daily routine for the balance of my life. I head to the training table, grab a Styrofoam container filled with my dinner, and head upstairs to my office to make some recruiting calls before we start our offensive staff meetings for the evening. It's amazing that you can do this, day after day, and it becomes so ingrained in you that you think it is normal. It's why so many coaches have trouble in normal social settings. They don't really function outside of this cocoon. After a while, this seems more normal to me than going home.

I make a quick call to Cyndy to say hi and ask if I can stop over to see her tonight after the meetings. Nothing like calling a girl you just started dating and ask if you can stop by at 10 p.m. that night. It already creates the wrong impression. "Why 10, do you have another date first?" she teases. Honestly, it is like she is too good to be true! She instinctively seems to get it in every way. "Yes, a date with a bunch of grumpy, fat old men who are going to spend the next three hours bitching about a bunch of college kids," I respond. She laughs. "See you when you get here," and hangs up.

It is interesting to me as a young coach to watch this dynamic. About half the staff is on wife number two or three. The other half has a tight relationship with their spouses, in some cases as close as I have ever witnessed. As a coach, advancing your career is a team effort, and generally those with the best relationships tend to rise in the business faster. This is a tough life on a marriage and you both better recognize what you signed up for (as my mom used to say).

I ring the doorbell to Cyndy's apartment and she greets me wearing nothing, and I mean nothing, but a Birmingham State football jersey. She is the most beautiful woman I have ever seen in my life! "I thought maybe you could teach me a few things from practice today," she giggles. I just met the woman of my dreams and I am the happiest man alive. We spend the rest of the night in each other's arms talking like we have known each other all of our lives. I just found the partner I need to make this all work.

CHAPTER 6

RECRUITING

I actually enjoy recruiting. A lot of coaches don't. Maybe it's because I am young and relate well to the players, but I enjoy being in and out of schools, driving or flying from one town to the next. I like trying to discover the player who the other schools might have missed. With all the national recruiting services, you have to be careful not to recruit a player just because he sounds or looks good.

In Alabama, they like to say there are three seasons. The football season, the recruiting season, and spring practice. Sometimes, it seems like the recruiting season is the biggest of them all. CEOs of companies take time out of their busy days to follow the latest news on recruiting on various websites. It seems a little strange to me, but if that is what excites them, so be it. That does mean the pressure to deliver in recruiting is immense. That's why people cheat. One or two players can change the whole perception of your recruiting class and that excites the fans.

I have never cheated in recruiting, so all of this is new to me. What I really never would have expected, is how well organized the process is. There are always rumors flying around that this school or that school cheats. That one coach or another is buying players. Yet, very seldom do schools ever get caught. It proves to be very low risk to cheat and the benefits are enormous, both for the school and the head coach. But success impacts everyone in the organization, not just the head coach. For me, being on a winning coaching staff will give me a chance to be a coordinator at a bigger school. For our coordinators, it might give them a real chance to be a head coach and earn millions. To a large extent, you are all tied together by a common bond of a desire to win, for a multitude of reasons, not just the competitive part.

I am in a very unique and uncomfortable situation because I am dating the daughter of our largest recruiting benefactor. He seems to be fine with my dating his daughter, but his role in the recruiting process is all business. He is laser focused on doing his part.

Here is how it works. I decide who we are going to recruit in my assigned recruiting area and the other coaches do the same thing. Once we have all of our lists made, we decide, as a staff, after watching their game film, in what priority order we are going to recruit the various players. When that is complete, our recruiting coordinator, Jimmy Dykes, has a private meeting with Gary Waters, where he learns about every player on the recruiting board. Gary takes very detailed notes on each of the top players. His mission then is to figure out what boosters in the various towns where these players live are loyal enough to Birmingham State to "help" in the recruiting process. You have to be extremely careful, so someone who already knows the player is the best. Once that is figured out, Gary and his group go to work.

It is strange to me. I am recruiting the players just like normal, knowing all the time there is something else going on in the background. The players probably think it's a little weird, but they understand why I cannot have any knowledge of it.

Then it comes time to pay homage to our benefactor. One by one each assistant coach goes to Gary's office for a private luncheon. It's pretty nice, the top floor of the bank building, forty stories up, in a small dining room reserved for the President. As I push the button to head to the 40th floor, I wonder how much time we will spend on recruiting, and how much time on my personal life?

As I exit the elevator, a pretty blonde woman greets me and says, "Welcome Coach. Mr. Waters is waiting for you in the dining room." The minute I step through the door, he pops up and greets me like a long-lost friend. "Glad you could be here (like I had any choice). Whadda ya think, pretty nice up here, isn't it? The view is great. I like to say you can see every corner of Alabama from here."

"Thank you for having me, sir. I have never been to a place quite like this," I say carefully.

"Let's knock off the 'sir' stuff, even if you are dating my daughter," he laughs. "She really likes you, so treat her right."

"I intend to, sir. I like her a great deal as well," I say sincerely.

"Well let's get down to business," Gary barks. "Tell me about these guys you are recruiting. Seems like you are on some good ones." From that point, it is all business and Gary takes very detailed notes. He wants to know every little thing about each player that I am recruiting. I can tell he is good at this. He wants to leave no stones unturned and that is good. When we finish, we both stand, shake hands, and are off to our regular business. It all seems very casual to me, but they have a system.

This is a process to be repeated again and again. We don't get all the recruits, but we get our share. The competition is stiff, but you need to at least get your share of the good ones if you want to win. You never quite know if it is you, the school, or something else that will finally secure the commitment from the player. But at some point, you realize it doesn't matter. He's coming to your school and that was the goal.

As I head into my first full recruiting season, I want to make a statement by getting at least one player that others would say I can't get. It is going to be hard work, but I think I can make it happen with a player named Adrian Brown, the top running back in the state of Alabama. He goes to Gadsden High School in Gadsden, Alabama. The school is well known for a wealth of football talent, but even there he is special. He will be recruited by Alabama and Auburn, of course, but he is an NFL player in terms of talent, and he will be an early entry into the NFL draft. My hope is that he will see that he can play right away for Birmingham State. These other schools have stockpiled running backs. No matter how good he is, he might be hidden for a year or two. If we can convince him to come to Birmingham State, we will help him amass so many yards he is sure to be the first player selected in the draft. At least that will be my pitch to him. I like high stakes games and this is going to be one. If I can deliver, I will instantly make a name for myself in this business.

So, off I go in pursuit of Adrian Brown. All I need is a chance, some good luck, and a little help from Gary Waters and the gang. I forgot to mention the other factor in my favor. Adrian comes from a very, very low-income area. While he is likely to one day make millions of dollars in the NFL, today his mom will have trouble paying the light bill. If there is one thing I know, quality young men always want to take care of their mothers. They can't stand to see their moms suffer and if there is a means to address that, they will. Three years waiting for an NFL contract is a long time. Help now would mean a lot.

Now, I'm not the only one who knows that, so the competition will be stiff. I just have to hope I can win the other factors, and then match what other schools will offer.

CHAPTER 7

ADRIAN BROWN

It is now noon and I am sitting in Gadsden High School waiting to see Adrian Brown. I have been at the school since 8 a.m. today, talking to the football coach, the principal, teachers, custodians, cafeteria workers, just about everyone in the school. I have always figured that if others at the school like me, they might just tell the prospect that I'm a good guy. You never know for sure who has influence with any particular player. The more people with whom you connect, the better. Any little advantage I can find is key to ultimately closing the deal.

The people here are really nice and in a community like this, the star player on the football team is a pretty big deal. It seems odd that would be the case, but even the most successful businessmen in town want to know a player like Adrian. It is one of the special things about sports, I guess. People are just drawn to the stars. Generally, this goes one of two ways. The player becomes a complete jerk and takes advantage of everyone, or he remains a solid person and his legend grows to new heights. In general, the first one always has a sad ending, probably predictable.

Fortunately, Adrian falls in the second category. I have not been able to find anyone who does not just love the kid. He is mature, respectful, appreciative, and people seem to gravitate to him. It appears for 17 years old, he is already very politically savvy, which must be an inherited trait. It is almost amazing to watch as he comes down the hallway of the high school, shaking hands with some, hugging some, with a big smile on his face. It is as if he were running for office where he would win in a landslide.

As he enters the office, he first greets his coach, Joe Bob Sagan, with a firm handshake and says, "hello sir." "Adrian, I want you to meet the coach from Birmingham State. He's been here all day, anxious to meet you," says Coach Sagan.

"It's a pleasure to meet you, sir. I apologize for making you wait so long. I have been in classes all day and just got out," Adrian says.

"I'm thrilled to meet you, Adrian. I have been at the school all day long and everyone here has so many nice things to say about you. Your mother must be very proud," I start.

"I hope that she is, sir. Thank you for saying that," he responds. You only get certain spots in this business and I wanted to open by immediately talking about his mom. She is his North Star. Here is the reality, I'm not even supposed to be talking to him. The NCAA rules don't allow it. But I can tell you no one follows the rules. Every coach knows the other schools are breaking the rules, but he just doesn't say anything.

Adrian and his coach know this as well. If an NCAA investigator comes to the school to ask questions, everyone will deny that anyone talked to anyone. That is how the game is played. In the end, no one got an advantage because everyone was treated the same.

"I wanted to be here the very first day of spring recruiting so you know you are the No. 1 player on our board. If Coach Jackson were allowed to be here, he would be standing right next to me. That is what you mean to Birmingham State football," I continue.

"I always liked Birmingham State and Coach Jackson wins all the time, so I like that," Adrian explains.

"I am going to start calling you regularly and we want to get you to campus this summer to spend the day with us. Maybe, even have you come to summer camp if you can," I say.

"I'd like that sir. Thank you for coming by to see me," he says. At this point the meeting is over. You can't get greedy when you aren't even supposed to be talking in the first place. It was a good first meeting and he didn't seem to hesitate in his interest. You can usually tell right off the bat if a player has no interest in your school. Recognizing interest is important, so you don't waste time recruiting a player you aren't going to get anyway. The best recruiters zero in on the targets they believe they can sign and move on from those they cannot. I want to be the guy who focuses on the right players and then closes the deals.

As I leave the school, my first call is to Coach Jackson to tell him I think it all went well. The second call is to Gary Waters, who is just as interested, maybe even more, on how things went. "He says he has always liked Birmingham State," I tell Gary. He responds, "then let's see if we can make him like it even more!" For some reason, I just like this guy. He is always positive and upbeat, and I always feel better after talking with him.

The next call is to Cyndy. I haven't been able to see her as much as we both would like. Spring ball was intense and then we headed right into spring recruiting. Like her dad, she is always such a spark when I call to talk with her. "Are you calling to tell me you met some good-looking woman in Gadsden?" she kids. "I didn't even notice if there were women in Gadsden," I answer back. "Oh, you are a good recruiter, maybe a big liar too. So how did it go? Is this the kid who will make you famous and move me out of Alabama?" She asks. "I think it was a good start, he is a great kid. I will need you on this one. He will really like you and you can make him feel comfortable," I add.

A lot of coaches don't get this. Kids get tired of coaches and they want a break from them once in a while. A wife or girlfriend with a warm personality can make recruiting much easier. The player will tell her things he would never say to me. As I said, Cyndy will be a great partner and a true asset as we move through this business. She gets it, and she wants to be a part of it. Lucky for me.

After two weeks, I begin to call Adrian to build a relationship. He always takes my calls and we always have a nice conversation. I plan ahead for any call, focus on what the topic will be, and what result I want to achieve. Kids don't want you to waste their time. If they want to shoot the breeze with someone on the phone, it will be their friends, not a football recruiter.

My first calls are focused on getting Adrian to campus for summer football camp. We already have it arranged that Jim Augustine, who has a son on the team with Adrian, will bring both players down. Adrian does not have the money for camp, but Jim is a good Birmingham State alum and fixes that. When he suggests that the players go to camp together, Adrian tells him he doesn't have the money to pay for it.

"Why don't you come over to the house on Saturday. I have a few projects that could use your help. I will pay you and that should just about be the amount needed to pay for camp," says Jim. "That's very nice of you, Mr. Augustine," says Adrian.

That night when I call Adrian about coming to camp he says, "I'm all set. I am coming down with a friend." Isn't it amazing how a little back door preparation can create a good result?

"Fantastic! I am going in right now to let Coach Jackson know you are coming down," I say. Getting him on campus is huge, and a big story in Alabama. He is the No. 1 player in the state so everything he does is noticed and written about. We are already making some waves with this story out there.

When he arrives at camp, he probably feels a little smothered. Every coach is falling all over himself to be his buddy. I know I am young, but I have a pretty good feel for this. That is not what he wants. I am going to keep my relationship with him very casual and try not to over-recruit him. I think he will see through the other stuff, at least I hope so.

That evening Cyndy comes down to campus to say hello. It has been hard to see her this week so dinner at camp seems like a date. This is the perfect chance to have her meet Adrian.

"Cyndy, this is Adrian Brown. Adrian, this is my girlfriend, Cyndy," as I introduce them. Like a pro, Cyndy says "Hi Adrian, where are you from?" Perfect! I want him to meet someone who doesn't know or care if he is a good player. Instantly, the two begin talking about everything imaginable. This lasts for the next hour and it could not have gone any better.

"If this dating thing doesn't work out, can I still use you in recruiting?" I joke. She slugs me in the stomach and says, " How much money will that kid make in the NFL? I think he really likes me." She can dish it right back and that makes this fun.

The summer months continue on and we seem to be holding our own with Adrian. He comes to a couple of our games, but he also visits most of the top schools in the south as well. However, there is something very easy about our relationship and he seem to be very open with me.

One night when I call, Adrian says, "Coach, you can't tell any- one else, but I think I want to come to Birmingham State. I just worry about my mom and want her to be alright." Bingo. Here is where we head toward the goal line. "Adrian, that is terrific news. You don't need to worry about your mother. I know she will be taken care of while you are here," I counter. "Let's just keep it quiet for a while. Don't even tell Coach Jackson just yet," he asks. "You got it, trust is everything, Adrian," I reply.

I hang up the phone on an adrenaline high. This is the guy I need to make a name in this business. I immediately call Gary Waters. "I know it is late, but do you mind if I come by the house?" I ask. "Come right over son, you sound excited," he says.

As I head to his house, I realize that as big as this is, I just made a decision from which there is no turning back. I can rationalize cheating in my mind, but it's still a step across the line from which I can never return.

All that is left is for Gary and his group to do their part, and the deal is complete. This will be the recruiting story of the year, and I will be one of the greatest beneficiaries.

CHAPTER 8

WHAT'S NEXT?

After three full seasons at Birmingham State, I am now married to the girl of my dreams, Cyndy. We have won three conference titles in a row, and I have established a pretty good reputation as a coach and recruiter. In this business, that means it is time to move on.

One thing you need to know about coaching is the myth of staff continuity. Every coach will tell you how important it is to have continuity to be successful. It is good to not have to re-train coaches all the time and players get comfortable with the same assistants, but the reality is this, those who stay at the same place just can't get out. If you have nine assistants, the bottom four or five just aren't really talented enough to get a better job somewhere. That is probably okay because it is the top half of the staff that makes the difference.

There is always one guy on the staff who is tracking every possible job opening. If you want to know what opportunities are out there, he's the guy to talk to. In our case, it is Jack Farmer. He is on the phone every waking hour tracking the job market.

"So, what do you hear, Jack," I ask innocently. "There is going to be a lot of movement this year, especially in the Power Eleven. You should be in a great position being from Ohio," he responds.

It does seem logical for me to head north to broaden my reputa-tion and experience. Cyndy has never lived in the north, but she is game for anything. This seems like the right time to make a move. I make a few calls to guys I know, just to get my name in the mix for any open jobs. By this time, Adrian Brown is the country's leading rusher, a likely Heisman Trophy winner as a junior, and a certain first round NFL draft choice. That alone will get me some attention as an assistant, but I need to sell myself a little to the public.

A couple of days later, I get a call from the director of football operations at McNally University in McNally, Michigan. He asks if I would be interested in a job there as the run game coordinator. That's becoming the thing now, schools get you to move for a newly created title and more money. They already have an offensive coor-dinator so they can't offer me that. It sounds pretty appealing actu-ally. A Power Eleven job, nearly double my current salary, near my hometown, and a school that has had reasonable success. I don't know the head coach, but he is fairly well respected. I tell him I'd like to talk it over with my wife tonight. That is coaching ritual. You always start by saying you want to talk it over with your wife. This makes you seem very human. Of course, you have already had this conversation with your wife fifty times and, as long as the money is good, she is on board. A coach's wife has to be ready to move and move often.

The hard part is telling Coach Jackson. He has been good to me and gave me a chance, but I have also done a good job for him. I think most everyone would say I am the best recruiter on the staff and my players have played well on the field. In three years, I have recruited 15 players and all but two of them are now starters. I like Coach Jackson and would stay attached to him if I thought he was going to move, but they take really good care of him at Birmingham State and he likes it here. A lot of guys, if they are making good money, should realize when they have a good thing going and stay put.

He isn't really too surprised when I tell him I am flying up to talk to McNally University. He moved a fair amount early in his career, so he gets it. That doesn't stop him from making an attempt to keep me. "If it's about money, I can talk to people here and I am pretty sure we can give you a big boost," he counters. "It's really not that, Coach, although they are being pretty aggressive on salary. I just think I need some additional experience, in another league, in a different part of the country. You have been great and I have learned so much from you in a short time. But one day I want to be a head coach, so I am trying to position myself for that to happen," I add.

"The hardest part will be your father-in-law, but you let me handle that one. Both of you might need a little distance anyway," he laughs. "Just be ready when Cyndy calls home and tells her folks she is freezing to death and you are never home," he adds with a little underhanded jab.

He's right. To this point it has really been pretty easy. Even with my crazy schedule, Cyndy still has her family and all her friends. Honestly, the life of a coach's wife is lousy in most respects. You get to be part of a lot of excitement and the pay is pretty good, but you also experience tremendous disappointment and, in general, become an expert at packing and moving. It's not a great life for a lot of people, but once you get on that track, it is what you signed up for. I hope Cyndy still thinks this is good a few years from now.

I asked if Cyndy can come along to Michigan to see the place and meet the people, a process I will repeat all of my professional life. Not only is she moving too, but she has the best people instincts I have ever witnessed. Of course, she is only interested in what is best for me/us, and there is not another person on earth who I can completely trust. Others have a vested interest in the decision and they give you their best advice. However, it always tends to be tilted toward their own particular situation and needs.

The other funny thing about coaches is that if you ask one hundred coaches if you should stay or go, all of them will say to go.

It's just ingrained in the culture. You do a job to take another job. Other coaches don't even wait to hear what the job is before they tell you to go. I never cared much for the opinion of other coaches. I already know what they are going to say. These decisions have to be made in a carefully plotted strategy to get to the top. Luck plays a big part, but being in the right place at the right time trumps all. The decision in the next 48 hours is whether or not this is the right next step. As we board the plane in Birmingham, I am glad Cyndy is coming along. She will see things no one else will see.

When we land in Detroit, we are met by a nice young graduate assistant named Carl Samuels. His job is to drive us back to the hotel and get us settled before we start to meet anyone. It always kills me, this little dance that coaches do in assigning certain tasks. It seems odd that a school, recruiting you and your wife, would send the least senior person on the staff to pick you up. It's a little bit of a power play. An assistant coach gets to assign the task. For the G.A., it's a big deal to get to meet another coach. Maybe this will be his ticket to a full time coaching job. If you are a smart G.A., you volunteer to do everything because you never know where it might lead. Some guys don't get this, and they are the ones who gets stuck and can't find jobs.

Carl is a nice young guy. This is his first year as a G.A., but he played at McNally for Coach Oliford, the current head coach. Maybe it is the recruiter in me, but I can almost always get the young guys to talk openly. Carl was perfect.

"So how do you like coaching, Carl?" I asked to open. "I really like it. I think as a player I had no idea all that goes into coaching. I am sure getting an education," he says.

"Has it been strange to go from playing for Coach Oliford to sitting in the staff meeting room with him?" I dig deeper. "It's certainly different, but if you know Coach Oliford, he is as straight up as you can find. That's why all the players respect him and love playing for him. He doesn't have a phony bone in his body," he continues. "We win because of him and the players will tell you that. He is really terrific." Bingo! That is exactly what I want to hear from a credible source. I don't want to work for a phony. Eventually the players lump you into that same category.

Coach Jackson was an asshole, but he was not a phony. You can be any kind of personality, but as long as you are honest and direct, the players will always be fine. More than anyone else, the players are human truth detectors. Once you gain their trust, you are on the right track.

Cyndy chimes in, "What's it like to live up here? It seems really cold and isolated to me." Carl does not hesitate. "There probably isn't anyone on our team or coaching staff who wouldn't rather live in a warm climate. But we also know that each Saturday we will have 85,000 fans in our stadium. Football is a really big deal here. So, you wrap yourself in the good things and try to ignore the cold. It's really that simple." Pretty heady response from a young guy. He is impressing me more every minute. Carl doesn't know it, but he is impressing Cyndy even more and that will pay big dividends in the years to come.

As we near the hotel, it becomes pretty clear that Power Eleven schools are massive institutions. This one dominates the entire town. Football is a big deal here. "I don't think I have ever been to a city where the football stadium is the largest structure in town," Cyndy says. "Yes ma'am, and the place is jumping on Saturdays. It will make you forget all about the cold," Carl laughs.

We shake hands with Carl, thank him, and head up to our hotel room at the Marriott on campus. It's a nice place, not great, but very nice for an on-campus hotel. Cyndy and I look at each other. Maybe this will be our next stop. I guess we will know in about 24 hours.

That is another thing about this business. There is no long interview process where both sides have time to make a really good decision. Often times these decisions come at a moment's notice.

You decide in a day and move the following day. (Expediency in hiring seems to be more well regarded than the coach you are actually able to hire.) It is just the way it is.

The visit starts with a dinner with Coach Oliford and his wife, Mary Jane, at the best restaurant in town, a place called Dish. It's a small place and everyone knows the Olifords, of course, but they seem to know they are there on business and leave them alone. One young guy comes up and asks for an autograph for his dad. (They are never for them you know). Coach Oliford obliges in a very polite manner.

This feels so different to me. The last time I got a job, I was by myself, being demeaned by the head coach and begging for a job. Now, we are sitting with a highly-regarded head coach and his wife having a very professional dinner. About five minutes after sitting down, it is clear Cyndy is the star of the show. Both the Olifords are completely taken with her personality, intelligence, and energy. It is why everyone gravitates to her. I am perfectly fine with letting her carry the evening. My time with Coach tomorrow will be a totally different type of interview.

"Well, it seems to me you have way out-kicked your coverage with Cyndy," Coach Oliford says with the overused coaching jargon. "With all due respect, I was about to say the same thing about you, Coach," I answer back. He laughs, "I like that. I have often said that, without Mary Jane, I'd probably still be a graduate assistant at Monmouth College."

"I'll let you in on a secret, Coach. Adrian Brown liked Cyndy more than he liked me. She should probably get the credit for recruiting him," I say with a twinkle. I do this for two reasons. One, to answer back to his self-deprecating humor, and two, to remind him that I coached and signed the best player in the country. If you are going to succeed in this business, you have to be a self-promoter. Everyone had a style. Even those who insist they don't want the media spotlight, end up creating such a persona that not talking becomes their persona. It's all part of the game, and it really is a game.

By the end of the evening, I know they are sold on Cyndy and probably feel good about me. Tomorrow though, I have to get on the board and talk football. I'm fine with that. It's just stressful when a room full of assistant coaches try to make you look foolish. Their sole intent is to make themselves look better. The assistants will all pretend to have input on the new hire. The reality is the head coach decides and they all act like that is what they decided as well.

The offensive staff is a group of seasoned guys who have been with Coach Oliford since he took the job eight years ago. I would be the first "new guy" in a while. The idea of continuity is great and they have been winning, so the dynamic works for them right now. Like all staffs who have been together for a while, the coaching tends to get better but the recruiting tends to falter. Winning has a habit of making guys lazy. Coaches start speaking at Coaching Clinics and other outside speaking engagements for money. They do some coaching videos, write a book, all things that detract from time spent recruiting. The truth be told, this school needs a spark in recruiting so they keep enjoying the better times.

The session with the staff was about what I expected. They quizzed me on techniques and asked me about things we were doing at Birmingham State. Nothing out of the ordinary. I had the feeling they were told to go easy on me because Coach Oliford had already decided that he wants to hire me. That's fine, I am going to be spending a lot of time working with these guys if I take the job, so I better develop a good relationship with them.

The next session is with Coach Oliford himself, just the two of us, in his private conference room. (This is so different than what I had experienced at Birmingham State, as I mentioned.) This is such a dignified and professional man sitting across from me.

"So, what do you think after being here for a day?" he asks. "I can see this place is special," I begin. "And I like the people I have

41

met. I would imagine recruiting is a big challenge given the geography and population base in the north." He does not back away. "It is. That is part of the reason you are here. We need to recruit well, and you have had a lot of success. I think the difference here is you can really make a name for yourself, which will be a big career boost. What are your ultimate goals as a coach?"

I say very confidently, "I want to be a major college head coach and win the National Championship."

Coach Oliford smiles, "Not very many people have the courage to say that and certainly not with as much conviction. If you come here and help me, I will make sure I put you in a position to try and achieve those goals." This is what I like, direct and straightforward. You help me, I will help you. No coach-speak or glib phrases, just a straight business transaction.

"I like that, Coach. I would like to go back to Birmingham and think about it for a day. I also want Cyndy to feel very comfortable about this. You can see we are partners in this whole venture," I add.

"That's fine with me. I just don't want things to drag on too long," he says.

"It won't," I respond decisively.

When I meet Cyndy at the hotel and head to the airport, she is in good spirits. "It's different than what we are used to, but you can buy a really nice house at a great price," she says. "Wouldn't it be nice to have a great house where we could invite your players over for dinner once in a while?" Sometimes I am amazed by her thought process. She is already mapping out a strategy for success. It looks like we are headed to McNally University.

CHAPTER 9
EVERYTHING IS NEW

I t seems like when you start over at a new school, you spend the
first month just figuring out how to get around. Especially when
you are the only new addition to the staff. Everyone else knows the
routine. You always feel like the odd man out.

This is also different for me because I am living alone at a hotel. Cyndy will be arriving soon, but she is not here yet. The hardest part of the process was telling her parents that we were leaving.
I'm sure they always figured eventually we would move, but I'm
also sure they hoped it would not be so soon. Gary handled the
news better than her mom. She was not happy about our move.
Taking her daughter and possibly future grandchildren to another
job a long way away did not make me a very popular guy. I left it
up to Cyndy to help bail me out of this one and she did a good
job of convincing them it was a joint decision. She is firmly committed to pushing me forward in this business. I am not sure she
totally knows what she signed up for, but right now she is strong
and focused. I think she wants a new adventure and getting away
from the shadow of her parents appeals to her. It's also a little uncomfortable for me currently because Gary is so directly involved
at Birmingham State. At some point that will become an issue. It is
best for everyone to move forward in another direction.

Since I am living alone in a hotel, I end up just staying at work late and then heading back early in the morning. It's actually a good way to get started right and to learn as much as I can quickly without feeling any guilt to "get home." There is so much to learn, especially the football part, since these guys have been together a long time.

Fortunately for me, the tight ends coach is a fantastic guy. His name is Bud Placek. He immediately takes me under his wing and makes sure the transition is smooth. I'm not really sure why, he is just a good guy, it appears. The other guys are fine. They just aren't going to go out of their way to make me feel welcome. I also think Bud is different because, from what I can tell, he is probably the best recruiter on the staff.

In addition to football, we talk a lot about recruiting and what it takes to be successful at McNally University. I need to get a good handle on what it takes to be successful here. It becomes pretty clear that they get "help" from local businessmen to land the top recruits. It is just done in a much more low-key manner than in the south. They have a group they call "The Coaches Crew." These guys gather regularly to talk about recruiting and support the program. Unlike how we did it at Birmingham State, The Coach's Crew take matters into their own hands after hearing the overall report on how recruiting is going. I think it seems much more dangerous this way, because you have people out on their own, doing what they think is best. However, it does put greater distance between the coaching staff and illegal activities should they get caught. However, the biggest competitors are all doing the same thing, so it is unlikely you will get turned in for violations. The great thing about the Power Eleven is that the schools espouse all these high ideals and academic integrity, yet they are cheating just like everyone else. I get it, and I have already gone to the dark side, so it really doesn't bother me anymore. There is always the burden you carry of getting caught and damaging your career, but any more, even that doesn't seem to be a great risk. I just need to be smart and keep control of the situation as it relates to my own recruits. I get the impression that the methods here are a little more sophisticated, so we all go about our business pretending this doesn't even happen.

"Tell me about The Coach's Crew," I ask Bud. He laughs and says, "necessary evil. They are really kind of a pathetic group, trying to be on the inside of the program and chasing 19-year old kids for autographs. That is just part of our business, I guess. I just try and be cordial and not get too close. It's really Coach Olifords group anyway."

So, that is the biggest difference. The head coach orchestrates this, which means that we are supposed to play ignorant. It is kind of funny when you think about it. It's no different than the CEO of a big company who claims to stay above the fray, but knows every dirty trick going on in his business. Cheating starts at the top in college football, just like it does in business. The difference is when a CEO gets caught, he ends up in prison. All that is really at stake in college football is reputation. The reputation of the coach and the reputation of the school. But generally, you find out that everyone at the school is in on it, from the Board of Trustees on down. Weak Presidents are never going to cross their Boards, so it becomes a big game. McNally is no different from the rest. For the coach, it can damage him for a period of time. Then some school decides they want to win, so they hire him and claim he is a changed man. Laughable!

Bud is really good about getting me connected around campus as well. His wife, Toni, is very nice and she has been just as great getting Cyndy situated with the move and anything she needs. That makes a big difference in a move like this because I am so busy all the time. Sadly, I have little time for Cyndy.

The other thing that seems different from the outset is that people want to do things for you. People invite you to use their vacation homes or homes on the lake. One guy does all your dry cleaning for free. A dentist takes care of you for free. Another guy offers free car washes. Each year a group takes the coaches and their wives on a cruise. It all sounds great but there is always a motive, and being close to the coaches and players is their purpose. At the beginning, it all seems great, but then you start to feel like they own you.

As you move through this business, it starts to become real on every level. Yet it isn't real. You don't really develop friendships, you just develop a group of people who you need and they need you. It's all part of the deal and why they often say, "it's why you get paid the big bucks."

Different from what I had experienced at Birmingham State, there are a whole series of events in the spring that I'm expected to attend. The purpose is to shake hands with big donors, and tell them about the team and recruits. It's all part of the "big time." These events are also the first time I experience the "groupies", often times wives of prominent donors, who want "to know the coaches." It all seems pretty creepy at the beginning, watching people make complete fools of themselves at these events. But the long-time coaches on the staff seem to have it down to a science. The husband sits at the bar, having way too much to drink, listening to the strength coach brag about how strong the team will be this year. (Guys love to hear all that stuff, even though we say it every year.) While the donor is totally engrossed, his wife is in the back room at the hotel, on her knees in front of the quarterback coach. At first, I kind of laugh about all this stuff. It is very well known and accepted among our coaching inner circle. Eventually, it becomes so common place you don't really even think about it.

Right now, I am a young married guy, and getting plenty at home. For these other guys, this is like another sport, and they are not going to miss an opportunity. And really, the women are freaks. They are not looking for a new husband, just looking for excitement, and this is the place to come. That's what I am referring to when I say it all becomes real. I am starting to think that all this stuff is normal. How sad is that?

The longer I am in the business, abnormal things become normal, like never being home. I am busy, I have meetings all day long with either coaches or players, it dominates my existence. For Cyndy, this is a hard adjustment. I moved her to a small town, in the north, with no friends, no job, and I'm gone seven days a week. She is being a good sport, but I can tell it is starting to get to her. I have her come down to the training table once in a while for dinner, or maybe stop by at the end of practice, but it's not long before some of the older coaches suggest that is not a great idea. If their wives find out that Cyndy is down here, then they will start coming around, and the coaches don't want that. There are too many "things" going on to have their wives around regularly.

The football part of this has actually come together fairly easily. I have worked hard to prepare, and I think every year in this business, the coaching gets easier. We have smart players, and they already understand that they have to work hard and be knowledgeable to have real success. You also find that the players warm up to you pretty quickly. I think most kids just want you to be real with them. Don't try and sell them, just talk to them. They also know that they need you to get to where they want to go, the NFL. If they think you can get them there, they will really buy in. The academic stuff, that's a good PR line and sounds good in commercials, but the reality is, most of the players could care less about a college degree. They want the NFL, so as a coach, you have to sell that every single day. If you think about it, what better motivation than the chance to make millions of dollars right out of college? That is real, even though only a handful of these guys will ever make enough money playing football to feed their families. Try telling them that at age 20-21!

My job at McNally University is simple. Recruit great players and get the most out of them on the field. If this happens, we all benefit.

CHAPTER 10

FIRST GAME

For any coach, the first time you are a part of something is special and you never forget the feeling. I felt that way running onto the field at John J. Smith Stadium for our home opener against Ball State. Even though these are what we call "buy games," meaning the athletic director paid an opponent a large sum of money to come play one game in our stadium for the sole purpose of chalking up a victory, it still has a special feel.

For me, this is also the first time in a game with major coaching responsibilities. The title of run game coordinator means I will be calling some of the plays, a first for me. Our offensive coordinator is an overweight, dopey acting guy who never finishes a sentence or a thought, but seems to coach quarterbacks fine and has a good reputation. He played at McNally, though he was a fourth team tight end. He is an insecure guy who plays the role of the good old boy, but he is really a backstabber. I watch him all the time because I know he would like me to fail. He is in a unique situation though. Everything we do on offense will also reflect on him, so we both have to "play the game" to some extent. If you remember, he is also the one sneaking off to a back room with a donor's wife. He is, basically, a low-class guy. But if

I want to reach my goals, I need to make sure I use Pat Click to help me get there.

In a lot of places, the fans really don't pay attention to the assistant coaches. But at a place like this, they know every coach and what we each do, so they will be evaluating me today as well.

The excitement of the stadium is high for a game against an average team. The expectations for the season are probably unrealistic, but that goes with the territory. Right now, the fans believe we will go 12-0 in the regular season. But who would want to coach at a place with either low or no expectations?

I am going to be sending in the plays from the sideline. That may not seem like such a big deal, but for me it means a lot of "airtime" on the television broadcast and a lot more notoriety than I have ever had. It is all part of getting to where I want to go.

I also experience another head coach's style as we prepare for a game. Coach Oliford has a much different style than I am used to. He is very businesslike in the way he approaches the game and the preparation for the game. There is no yelling and screaming, just a very focused, methodical approach to the game. His belief is that you win the game during the week of preparation, not by getting all fired up on Saturday. It has been very interesting to watch how he approaches game preparation.

Following each game, we spend Sunday morning watching the film from the previous day's game. We watch it individually to grade the performance of each of the players we coach. Then we gather as a staff to watch the entire game, both offense and defense together, to get a complete view of the game. Coach Oliford is very hard on the assistants during these sessions, making us accountable for every good or bad play by our players. Once that is over, we break into offensive and defensive staffs to watch it again together for a further critique. This is an intense time. But, once we are finished, we will forget about this game, with the exception of watching the film the following day with the players.

The players have Sunday off, which I think is good for many reasons, not the least of which is getting a break from all of us. When you hear the same thing over and over again from the same people, it tends to get old. I know they tire of the constant pressure put on them by the coaches. It is also good for them to rest and heal for 24 hours. Football is a brutal game and the body needs time to recover. Sunday is that day for our players.

The rest of Sunday, we spend watching film of next week's opponent and preparing for practice. Sunday night is a late night, but I also discover it is a good day to slip out late afternoon to see your girlfriend, if you are one of the coaches who keeps a few of them around. I guess I am a little surprised that, in a small town, they can be so casual about it with their wives living ten minutes away. What I was shocked to find out is that, after the Cotton Bowl two years ago, some of the alumni bought the coaches a house where they can take their "friends" when they want to meet. That was the reward for a good season.

Jimmy Sax, our director of football operations, keeps the key and makes sure couples aren't there at the same time. Coach Oliford doesn't seem to use the house, but clearly knows about it. Despite his simple image, he seems to have a thing for girls in their 20s, which is amazing since he is 55 years old. It is kind of a joke among the staff, but we all pretend like we know nothing about it. The sick part is, he has two daughters about that same age. Oh well, I will go on about my business and try not to judge.

As we get ready to head out of the locker room for the final time before kickoff, you feel a complete calm come over the room as Coach Oliford asks the players to take a knee and say a prayer. When we are finished, it is like we have unleashed a bunch of wild men. They head for the door ready to pounce on the Ball State players. It sure feels like we are ready. I know I am.

My first chance comes in the middle of the first quarter, when we have the ball third down and three yards to go at the 40-yard line. We have not been able to sustain much of a drive so far so this will be our first chance to get something going. Pat Click wants to throw the ball. I decide to step in. "We need to run this right at them and make a statement. Our group needs confidence. We can pound the ball right at them and get momentum going in our direction." Pat says, "Listen rookie, we are going to throw the ball." I fire right back, "You are sending a bad message. Run the ball." Coach Oliford now steps in. "I want to run the ball and establish the line of scrimmage. Call the play." Like that, I am now officially accountable for the result. I call an isolation play and we crush the line of scrimmage for five yards. First down and the momentum shift is obvious. Nothing zaps the energy of a defense like knowing they can't stop you running the football. Once you gain control of the line of scrimmage, you just have to be smart and the results will follow.

We take the ball down the field and score and the rout is on. All in all, it is a great way to start the season.

As we head to the locker room after the game, Coach Oliford runs up from behind, puts his arm around me and says with a smile, "Nice call, rookie, keep being yourself." It was nice compliment and a good feeling after a win.

When I get to the locker room, it's not quite the same reception. "Listen you little prick, don't you ever make me look bad again," says Click. "I am just doing my job. It's not personal, it's just business," I respond. I am not going to take any grief from this guy. If I back down now, I will be doing it my whole career and that is just not me. He storms off and I know he will be out to get me, but I am smarter than he is so "game on."

When I leave the locker room, Cyndy is waiting for me. We all head over to Kevin Collier's house, our defensive coordinator.

He and his wife always host a postgame party. They are very nice people.

I tell Cyndy the story of what happened during the game. She just laughs and teases, "You little prick, how am I supposed to be friends with all these wives?" We both laugh knowing that this is just a stop along the way as we build toward the big prize. For the first time, that goal starts to seem real to both of us.

CHAPTER 11

OWNING RECRUITING

The biggest mistake a coach can make is to start thinking that coaching is the difference between winning and losing. Certainly, you need to be a good coach, but the ones who never forget that you need great players are the ones who win Championships. I have tried to never lose sight of that fact, even though it becomes harder and harder, the bigger the school. I can already see that some of the coaches on this staff have lost their focus in recruiting. They start to think that if they come up with some brilliant game plan in the film room, that will make up for not recruiting well. I have observed that some coaches don't want to be part of the reason you win, they want to be THE reason you win. That is just not the case. Great players make great coaches.

McNally University is going to be interesting for me because recruiting in the north is different than recruiting in the south. Each coach has an assigned recruiting area. Mine is Georgia, Florida, and any other great player in the Southeastern part of the United States. I am also going to be assigned some of the top offensive prospects to recruit, anywhere in the country. These are the guys who are the real difference makers. When a school can sign only 25 players, I believe it is the last five guys signed who make a recruiting class either great or average. My job is to find some way to sign those last five great ones.

Most of the rest of the recruiting class will come from the Midwest or East Coast. That's really where McNally is better known. The Southeast has been a struggle for us, in large part because the guy they had recruiting there before me was not very good. He was lazy and liked to chase around every night on the road. His popularity in Georgia and Florida was more among divorced women than high school coaches and players. That means I have a lot of work to do. But with the success of the team in recent years and some hard work, I will find some key players who will make a big difference.

The number of skill players in the Southeast, both in terms of speed and talent, is significant. There are just a lot of football players in this part of the country and the population base is growing. The Power Eleven has been a league generally built on the running game, not real exciting football, but consistent. Getting some "game breakers" to McNally will make us a much greater threat on offense and more explosive on defense. Coach Oliford knows this. Sometimes I wonder if the other assistants do, but that's not my concern.

My concern is getting players here who can make a difference. Equally important, I need to continue to build my reputation as a recruiter. If I want to be a head coach, I have to be the full package.

Recruiting during the season is not easy. You have to find time to make recruiting calls and still get your job done. On Thursday night, you fly to your recruiting area so you can spend Friday seeing your top recruits. Then you fly back late Friday night to be there for the game on Saturday. It is a grind, but that is how you make a difference. When you tell a player that you are flying all the way from Michigan to Miami just to watch him play, it has an impact.

When I land in Miami, I immediately see all of the private planes from the League South schools, all decorated with logos and school colors. In the Power Eleven, no one does that, probably because we are all state schools who have to explain things like that to our state legislatures. In the South, the football coach is more powerful than the Governor. The Presidents of the universities are scared to death they might offend the coach and be out of a job. It is really very sad, but that's the deal. I hope to be in one of those coaching jobs one day and wield that power. I like the thought of the League South because they just ignore the rules and everyone knows it. There is no pretense (except in the public domain) about academics. Keep the players eligible is the battle cry, and not a lot more than that.

As I head to the stadium, my focus is on this one particular player, a wide receiver at Miami Kingwood High School. He is 6-5, 235 pounds, runs a 4.4 in the 40-yard dash, and has hands like Jerry Rice. This is a guy who would be impossible to cover. Where will you find a cornerback with his size and speed to line up against him? You won't!

When I get to the field, there must be coaches from 30 schools there to watch Ahmad Burresh play. He is the most dynamic player in high school football this season. If you think about all the big-name schools in college football, they are all here, dressed in their school colors, trying to make sure Ahmad sees them standing along the field. It is really very distracting and I can't imagine that the high school coach is very excited about taking all the attention away from his team and this game.

Coaches are pretty selfish when it comes to all of this. Our career goals move way ahead of any concerns for the kid, his team, or his coach. But there is really nothing the high school coach can do but make the most out of it, and maybe he can get himself a new job at the college level out of the deal.

I already know a lot of the coaches from recruiting against them when I was at Birmingham State. Some guys are new to me. One thing for sure, whoever gets Ahmad will be the hero at his school and the chances of winning big grows exponentially. Let's hope that coach is me.

It may be my imagination, but when the team runs onto the field for warm-ups, Ahmad appears to give me a wave and a wink. We have not seen each other except for one time in the spring in his coach's office at the high school. I am wearing one of those awful McNally University polo shirts. It's really kind of funny. I'm standing with a bunch of men, basically wearing the same shirt, made by either NIKE, adidas, or Under Armour, trying to act like we are different. Other than the color of the shirt, even the designs are the same for every manufacturer. In our khaki pants, we must all look very silly to the people in the stands observing us from afar.

Ahmad is everything I hoped he would be. He is lightning fast, catches with soft hands, he is strong, and he has an intimidating presence. He is a game changer in every sense. Now we have to figure out how to get him to McNally.

As I stand there watching, a guy walks up and slaps me on the back. "Hell of a player, isn't he?" the man bellows as he sticks out his hand. "Carl Samuelson, I am one of The Coach's Crew. I live down here in Miami. Coach Oliford said you would be coming down to-night." So, this is how it works. I do my part here, and I "get a little help from my friends", as they say. Okay, I guess whatever works. "He's a hell of a kid, too. I have had him over to the house several weekends to do odd jobs and things," Carl brags. I wonder what Ahmad got paid for those odd jobs, probably not minimum wage!

"He is a great kid," I respond. "And he would be a game changer for us." Carl says, "I am well aware of that, Coach Oliford reminds me of that every week when we talk." His arrogance is irritating and he wants to make sure I understand that he is a big shot with a direct pipeline to the head coach. Some of these guys are so pathetic. They are a big success in their own professions, making millions of dollars. But when they get around a bunch of coaches and players, they make complete fools of themselves.

Of course, he can't help himself, he just has to keep going. "Coach has a place in Naples near mine, you know. He loves to sneak down here from time to time to get away. That's how we became pals. I help him get a few players and maybe introduce him to some of the younger talent down here, and I don't mean on the football field." He laughs and slaps me on the back again. I'm sure Coach would love this guy telling me that he supplies him with young girls. What a jerk. He just has to establish with me right off the bat that he's a big deal. I also just found out not to tell anything that I don't want repeated. At first, I thought it was odd that Coach didn't tell me this guy was coming to the game, but it starts to make sense now.

"There are a few of us down here who just love the program. We take turns flying our jets up to the games, at home and on the road. We just can't get enough," he adds. "Even my wife is into it. She is almost a bigger fan than me." I wonder what the wife is doing while this guy and Coach Oliford are out with the young girls? I'll bet I can guess.

So, we have "help" down here, but it is still not going to be easy to sign Ahmad. This guy is being recruited by everyone, and I am trying to talk him into flying a long way from home to play in the cold. It's the same basic issue we face with all players in the South, but I will give him my usual line. "You can't avoid the weather if you want to play pro football. What if you get drafted by the Patriots, the Steelers, or the Giants? You better learn to play in cold weather early so you can have a long and productive pro career." It really is true, but I'm not sure how many kids either buy it or understand it at their age.

With a player like Ahmad, you can't leave anything on the table. You have to sell every possible strength. Additionally, with a player like this, it is easy for the human part of the equation to be forgotten. You start selling so hard that you lose sight of the fact that he is just a kid. This is all a little overwhelming no matter how savvy or mature he might be. We are fortunate that Ahmad has a great mom. She is one in a million and will have a more global view of the recruiting process. That really helps. You cannot expect a 17-year old kid to see the big picture.

I want to make sure I see her before I leave the game. It's not legal under the rules, but I know that at least half of these coaches will talk to her before they leave, so I can't afford not to have her see me. She doesn't know all the rules. She will probably assume that I am rude if I don't talk to her.

I wait until almost halftime to slip over and see her. Her name is Letisha and she is the warmest person you can imagine. I have talked to her on the phone only, but she hugs me like an old friend. "It's so nice of you to come all the way down here. Ahmad and I both appreciate it," she says. "We are excited to come up there for a visit next month," she continues. I am fired up because Ahmad had not completely committed to a visit yet in our conversations over the phone, but it looks like Mom just sealed the deal. "We can't wait either. We will have so much fun together that weekend. My wife, Cyndy, is also excited to meet you both. You'll like her," I say. "I'm sure of that. Thanks again for being here tonight. I'll tell Ahmad that we spoke," she finishes.

Well, that encounter alone was worth the trip. I am on a high as I board the plane to fly back. This is a first great step to landing the big prize.

Before we take off, I give Cyndy a quick call. "It's all yours from here. Let's see if you can pull another Adrian Brown for me," I say. "You know, I'm getting a little tired of making you look good," she teases. "I'll be waiting for you when you land."

Wheels up and we head back to Michigan with hopeful signs all around.

CHAPTER 12
THE LIFE

The life of a coach can quickly begin to feel like the movie "Groundhog Day", where everything keeps repeating itself over and over, day after day. In fact, days eventually mean nothing to you. A Tuesday seems no different than a Sunday. A Monday no different than a Friday, and so on.

You get up and leave the house before anyone is awake. You drive straight to the office and pour a lousy cup of coffee made by some graduate assistant. You head into the film room, in my case with the offensive staff, where you pick up where you left off the night before. The offensive coordinator runs the projector, and you all sit around the table and discuss all the things the players did wrong on every play in practice. It is not necessarily a very healthy environment, but it is what we do for a living. With the exception of getting up to take a restroom break, this will be my position for most of the day.

About 9 a.m. our director of football operations steps in to tell us that Coach wants to have a staff meeting. This same scene repeats itself every day of the week, even though we always meet as a staff at 9 a.m. It is the ritual.

I like to say we "meet to meet," and it is true. No one sits in meetings longer than football coaches. There is this feeling that if you're not meeting, maybe the opponent is, and will get an edge on you. None of it is probably true, but that concern makes it an issue.

The staff meeting is pretty routine. The trainer, Eli Whited, runs through a list of the injuries indicating who can practice and who cannot. This prompts some discussion among the coaches suggesting that some players are "milking" the injury a little. Nothing changes, it's just to make a point about some of the players. Then Dan Kannely, our strength coach, gives a report on the progress and attendance in the weight room. These are always upbeat reports where the strength coach tells you that everyone is working hard and following his direction.

Jan Carlson is our academic counselor. She reports on the class attendance and academic progress. I find that academic people are careful not to unload all the bad news at once. They tend to give a partial report, so it doesn't sound so bad. When a guy is doing poorly in school, it is usually the position coach who gets the brunt of the ire from the head coach. "Why haven't you been monitoring him better? Why am I just hearing about this now?" The academic counselor has to be a little careful. If he or she loses the trust of the assistant coaches, he or she is finished. The people held least accountable for all of this are the players. Their academic failures become the responsibility of someone else. It is not a good system. These same behaviors carry over into the rest of their lives, and it is not to their benefit.

Then we get to recruiting, where the lively discussions begin. We have a large board in the meeting room with magnetic tags for each recruit. The tags include all of the essential information. Coach Oliford likes to rank our likelihood to sign a player using percentages. It is a complete shot in the dark, but it is part of the routine. You have to be careful here. If you are too optimistic, you are held accountable for that. If you are too pessimistic, you are liable to be criticized for doing a poor job of recruiting. It's a crazy exercise, but part of the job.

When it comes to me, I know the question will first be about Ahmad Burresh, the wide receiver from Miami. I put the percentage chance of getting him at 25%, which is reasonably high for a player of this magnitude. I can tell that Coach Oliford is pleased that I am reasonably optimistic. "A guy like that can make the other 24 signees look pretty good," he says. "It was a good trip, Coach, but everybody else in the country was there also," I respond. "He has committed to a visit for the Illinois game, so that is a very positive sign."

There is an odd feeling in the room. I'm talking about a program changing type of player and it seems like half the coaches are jealous that I might sign him and put more pressure on them. It's the guys who have been in it a long time who seem to get pissed about the young, hard charging assistants on the staff. Maybe it is because they know the window has passed them by to do anything big. They are what they are going to be, assistant coaches. When I get to be a head coach, I will be aware of the young coach's enthusiasm and make sure I am encouraging it. I won't let the others discourage him. You have to have great players and passionate coaches to succeed.

After we finish the meeting, we go back into the offensive meetings and stay there until noon. That is when I get a break to work out and get something to eat. This is a key time for me to get recharged and ready for the afternoon practice. I usually go for a run and then lift some weights. I am determined to stay fit in a job where you can easily get horribly out of shape. The long hours become an excuse not to work out and then it goes from bad to worse. Nothing like having an overweight coach yelling at a player to get in shape. Pretty hypocritical.

In the afternoon, I make some recruiting calls to high school coaches to talk about players before I head into our player meetings.

The players' day starts with a team meeting run by the head coach. Coach Oliford is very good at this meeting. He always has a plan and is well prepared to focus the team for the day. I think a lot of coaches waste this meeting either by not being prepared or by missing the point of the meeting. This is your one chance each day to have your team's full attention and make sure the practice is not wasted. Otherwise, your only opportunity is yelling to your team on the field after practice. At that point, they are probably tired and not particularly interested in what you have to say. They just want to shower and eat. Young people have a short attention span, so make the most of it.

When we break from the team meeting, we head into position meetings with our players. Again, you have about 25 minutes with them. If you are not prepared, you waste time and it shows on the field. The little things make such a difference and preparation is the key to success. After these meetings, we head to the field. I love practice and time on the field. One coach used to say, "What other job do you get to put on workout clothes, run around outside, and have fun every afternoon?" I am of that same belief. This is a time where you build a special trust with your players. This is still teaching, it is just teaching football. How you instruct your players on the field will manifest itself in the game. If they are well prepared and they perform well, they will trust you completely.

When practice is over, it is dinner time at the training table and then back into staff meetings until about 10 p.m. You head home, go to bed, and then do it all over again the next day. The days all start to seem the same, because they all are the same.

Great for a family life.

CHAPTER 13

THE FAMILY

Cyndy is right. It is time for us to start a family. It just seems hard to imagine with my work schedule that I will be a good dad. I am very lucky. I had a great dad who was always there for us. He worked hard, but he never missed anything we did with a very few exceptions.

I watch a lot of college football coaches who have little or no relationship with their kids. I am determined that will not be me, but that will take a real commitment.

Cyndy has been a good sport with this move. She is a long way from family and friends and in a part of the country where she never thought she would live. Also, her husband is gone all the time, so she is alone a lot. It's not an ideal situation. In coaching, the assistant coaches' wives often become close friends. They can relate to the time demands and pressures of the job and they have a lot of events in common. It seems like games, recruiting dinners, and bowl trips bind them together as friends. This is a good thing in many ways. For someone like Cyndy, it gives her an instant group to hang out with. Without these women, she would only know random neighbors. This is the right time to start a family and another big step in our lives.

As the wife of a coach, Cyndy has been fabulous in every aspect. She seems to take to all of it so naturally, whether it is the recruiting part, cooking for the players at our house from time to time, or just talking one on one with a young player going through a tough time. She is a tremendous asset. She will be a great mother and I know I am very lucky.

We time the pregnancy so she will have the baby at the end of June, before we start the football season. It should make the transition a little easier, and hopefully I can be around to help for a while.

It is exciting to tell people that we are going to have our first baby. One of the first people, beyond family, that I let know is Ahmad Burresh's mom. I think this will make her feel close to us and provide another connection when they visit next week. She seems genuinely happy for us and even laughs and says, "Ahmad can babysit for you if he comes up there to school. He is the favorite babysitter of all my nieces and nephews," she tells me. I like everything about this woman. From our end, it may be Cyndy who ends up being the key. But believe me, before the weekend is out, we will make Ahmad and his mom believe our whole family can't wait for him to be part of everything we do.

When I tell Cyndy what Ahmad's Mom says, she laughs. "I love you, but I have been around your players long enough to know that I am never leaving our child with one of them." I laugh, and of course, agree with her. There are guys I have to call at 8 a.m. to make sure they get out of bed to go to class. Responsibility is not one of their greatest attributes.

I am recruiting Ahmad as aggressively as possible. I am also confident that Carl Samuelson and his buddies in The Coach's Crew are doing their part to help me out. I never mention this directly to Coach Oliford. It just seems like I am not supposed to. I also think if I told him I met Carl, he would wonder what else I know. I would rather not have that conversation. A lot goes unspoken in this business and that is probably for the best.

I have seen Carl and his buddies at some of the games. His wife is a very attractive woman and she seems to have "a thing" for our strength coach. The interaction between the two is strange. Carl is so busy chasing around on his own and falling all over Coach Oliford, he'll never notice. Maybe he really doesn't care. It is hard to tell with this kind of guy. I just try and keep my distance from all of it and do my job.

Cyndy, on the other hand, sees it all and wants to know what is going on. I'm not sure if it is out of curiosity, or defensiveness for the coaches' wives, but she is getting a little edgy. "Do you know what all these guys are up to?" she asks. "Honestly, I just try and stay out of it and ignore all this stuff," I respond. Cyndy says, "It's not right you know, and I feel like saying something."

"Okay, so here's the deal," I say. "What good will it do for us to get in the middle of it? We will just create a lot of enemies and we won't prevent anything anyway. We are just better to leave it alone."

"That's not how I was raised. These women are my friends and I feel obligated to tell them what I see," she says. "I get all that, but maybe they already know and you will just embarrass them further. I understand exactly what you are saying, but we have bigger things ahead and we just need to ignore it, and do our job. When we get to a place where we are in control, we can hire who we want and make an impact. This is just a stop along the way," I add.

"Okay, but it is such a strange feeling," she says. "Welcome to college football, Cyndy. This is my life every day," I say with a smile.

The arrival of Ahmad Burresh on campus feels like the Rolling Stones coming to town. Everyone knows he is coming and they all want to get some glimpse of him at the game, or in town over the weekend. It is pretty ridiculous when you think about it, all of this fuss over a 17-year old kid. But to a college football fan, one player can send the signal about the entire direction of the program. It is almost validation that the future will be bright, and you can believe that great days lie ahead for your team.

The same thing can happen with a new coach. But there aren't that many high-profile coaches you can hire who create the same spark that a great player does for the program. The energy surrounding a commitment from a big-time player is almost stunning.

For McNally, to get a player like Ahmad from Florida would be the ultimate coup. I am already getting a lot of credibility as a recruiter just based on the fact that he is taking a campus visit. It is also creating a little jealousy at work. No one likes the new guy getting too much credit. It doesn't help that the morning paper carried a headline that said, "As Good as Advertised," not talking about Ahmad, but about my recruiting. The story goes on to say that Coach Oliford brought me aboard to strengthen recruiting in part based on the success I had at Birmingham State. These things are all good for my career. They just aren't great for personal relationships. Even Cyndy is beginning to feel it from the other wives. The wives are competitive and one husband getting more credit tends to drive a wedge between them. Pat Click and his wife are always the worst. They are both passive-aggressive, in addition to not being too bright.

When I get to the office in the morning, I already know what is coming. "Glad you could join us this morning, Superman. We figured you would be doing TV interviews somewhere instead," Pat spouts. "Hey listen guys, I didn't ask for any of this, but if we get Ahmad, we will all look like Superman," I respond. That seems to kill the subject, but the pettiness just pisses me off. Click sits his fat ass in the office everyday doing nothing, while I coach and recruit. I think all this has passed him by and he knows it. I can't worry about that, I have my own goals to keep me focused.

I am really distracted today because I need this visit to be perfect. I have tried to think of every possible detail and hope I have it all covered. I meet with Jimmy Rayburn, a freshman running back from Miami, who I have asked to host Ahmad on his visit. Jimmy is a great kid and Ahmad knows him. They went to different high schools, but played against each other. Jimmy seems very happy here and I am his position coach, so I figure he will put our best foot forward.

I continually remind myself that the players are the key. If they don't believe in you or the school, you have no chance. I am hoping that Jimmy feels as good about McNally University as it seems.

I head out to the airport to pick up Ahmad and his mom. We were fortunate they had an open week in their schedule so he could come up for the game. I timed his arrival so he could be there for our Friday walk-through practice, and then go with the team to dinner and a movie. The guys on the team know he is coming, and I'm pretty confident they will do a great job.

I swing by the house to pick up Cyndy. She is waiting for me with a big smile and an energy that is completely infectious. "If we do this right, Ahmad may be our ticket on to bigger things," I say. "Let's just worry about this weekend and things will happen as they are supposed to," Cyndy warns.

When we greet them at the airport, there is a special feeling in the air. They seem excited to be here and we are thrilled to have them on campus. Cyndy and Ahmad's mom hit it off like fast friends. They never stop talking the entire ride back to campus. Ahmad and I have a nice conversation as we drive. We talk mostly about his team and how the season is going. He is really a terrific young man. There is something special about him. Even at 17 years old, you feel the potential for greatness from Ahmad.

When we get to campus, our players all greet Ahmad and his mom very genuinely. I can tell the Burreshs are impressed. What I had not counted on was Carl Samuelson and a few of his buddies at practice. Clearly this is by design, and okayed by Coach Oliford, but it still bugs me a little. I'd like to believe I can get Ahmad on my own, but the reality is I probably need a little help. How is he going to fly back and forth to Michigan with very limited financial resources? And, of course, how is his mom going to get to all his games? That's where Carl comes in. He is, as Bud Placek suggested, "a necessary evil."

Carl and his friends, of course, have to come over to say hello. It is clear they know Ahmad and his mom quite well, something that would not thrill NCAA investigators. It is also odd that a really attractive woman in her twenties is traveling with the group. Then I notice the chemistry between her and Coach Oliford. It seems that Carl has brought the coach a little present for the weekend. Of course, everyone acts like they notice nothing, with the exception of Cyndy, who rolls her eyes at me. The whole thing is sometimes surreal, but all I can do is vow that will not be me one day.

Ahmad's visit goes great, and we win the game fairly easily. That also means that everyone is in a good mood and attentive to making him feel very welcome. As I drive them to the airport on Sunday morning, I have a good feeling that I might be able to close this deal. It would be the biggest recruiting success in the history of McNally University.

CHAPTER 14

CLOSING THE DEAL

The longer I am in this business, the more I start to rationalize everything. I started with an idealistic view that I would play by the rules and show the world how it could be done the right way. Now I find myself turning a blind eye to things I never could have imagined, both personally and professionally. I know these things aren't right, but I have goals. Ultimately, I have to do whatever it takes to win. Winning is what matters.

I believe that once you make an exception, the next one is easier to make. In coaching, it is so easy to start convincing yourself that everyone else is doing it, so that makes it okay. Probably everyone else isn't doing it, but it sure seems like the winners are, and the chances of getting caught are just not that great anymore. "Better to get caught cheating and have to explain that, than to be a loser," it was once said. That seems to be a common notion today.

My goal right now is to get Ahmad Burresh to sign a "Letter of Intent" at McNally University. I already know what this is going to take and I'm prepared for that. For the first time, I'm not telling Cyndy what all is going on. We are going to have our first baby, a little girl, and I feel like I need to start protecting them from this. It is funny, but it didn't really strike me that way until Cyndy got pregnant. Now I am thinking that I don't want my little girl to think less of her dad.

Cyndy grew up with all of this. Maybe she didn't know everything, but she sure knew her dad was way too involved in recruiting. She is smart so she probably just tried to ignore it. But now we are a family, and I really don't want her exposed to all of this.

Cyndy is as driven as I am to succeed. She wants the "perks" that goes along with success in college football. She grew up in a wealthy family so is used to nice things. I think this makes her a willing partner in letting me do whatever it takes to get it done. I'm not sure what that means long-term, it just means today she is all in.

The baby will be great for her. She is focused on that right now while I head out recruiting. Her mom has come up from Alabama to stay with her, so that makes it much easier on me.

I am recruiting eight players and realistically, I think I can sign six of them. These eight players are among the very top on our recruiting board and I feel enormous pressure to sign the vast majority. Of course, most of my focus is on Ahmad Burresh, because he can make this class special and bring a lot of good players with him.

My first visit in his home includes Coach Oliford. We figured we might as well pull out the "big guns" right off the bat. When we get to the house, there must be fifteen people there. Aunts, uncles, friends, all wanting to meet Coach Oliford and be a part of the excitement around the recruitment of Ahmad. I can tell Ahmad is a little embarrassed by all of this. He really would prefer a quiet conversation with the four of us, but that is not to be the case. Often times this is the hardest part for recruits, separating themselves from the group that tends to follow them. Everyone is hoping that somehow this will also lead to money and a better life for them. That is a big burden for a 17-year old to carry. My hope is that this will work to our advantage with Ahmad. If he stays in Miami, this group will follow him everywhere. If he comes to McNally, he will be able to control his life on his own. (I am searching for any little edge that we might gain as we recruit Ahmad.)

Coach Oliford is very good in a home visit. He is not flashy, but comes across very sincere and genuine, which is most important. I can tell the assembled entourage is impressed. You don't often get famous head coaches into the lowest income parts of Miami. It feels like we made real headway on the visit. We leave the house and I drive Coach Oliford back to Naples where he is going to be for two more days. It appears Carl and his group have him well taken care of for the next forty-eight hours. I ask no questions, I just drop him off at the door. "You are doing a really good job. Keep it up. Your best days are still ahead," he tells me as he climbs out of the car. In many ways, I appreciate the way he approaches things. He knows what I want, and if I help him, he will respond by helping me when the times comes.

The issue with Ahmad is that every school in the country wants him. He has only visited McNally so far, and still has four other schools to visit. I still don't exactly know who our opposition is.

A few days later, Coach Oliford calls me on my cell phone. "Evidently Ahmad wants a commitment that he can start next year." Since I know Coach hasn't talked to Ahmad, this has to be coming from Carl. This is strange, but I guess that is how the negotiations will go. "What should I tell him Coach?" I ask. "Tell him, hell yes, he can start next year. We don't have anyone better," he responds. "And don't wait another hour to call him."

I hang up and dial Ahmad immediately. He answers the phone which is a good sign. If he didn't want to talk, or we were starting to lose him, he just wouldn't answer. "Ahmad, we had such a good time at your house the other night. Coach and I loved your family. What great people." "Sorry there were so many people here, Coach. They were just excited with both of you coming in and all," Ahmad says. "It was great. One thing Coach wants me to make clear, if we didn't the other night, is that if you come to McNally, we already have you in the starting line-up to open the season. You will also be wearing the jersey No. 1 that you requested," I continue. "That's pretty cool, Coach. Thank you. It's nice to hear." He's playing it cool, but it is clear he needed to hear that. (Thanks Carl).

I call Coach Oliford back on his cell phone to let him know that I have talked to Ahmad. "Maybe we can get this deal closed sooner rather than later," he says. "Should I be doing anything differently, Coach?" I ask. "No, you keep doing your part and let's see where this takes us," he finishes. In other words, there is more going on than I need to know, but that is okay if it all comes together.

The next few weeks are intense as Ahmad visits other campuses. I am finding it hard to sleep. But even after a visit to another school, he remains very positive and upbeat in our conversations.

On January 18, Ahmad's high school coach calls me to tell me that the next day, Ahmad is going to have a press conference to announce where he is going. He is not telling anyone before the press conference, except his mom. My reaction is that we are probably not getting him. I think he would let the winning school know in advance. I call Coach Oliford and update him, preparing for the worst. He is actually very upbeat and says he doesn't see this as a bad sign. Of course, he may have "inside information" that I don't.

At 3 p.m. the next day, with live television cameras and a room full of media, Ahmad Burresh pulls on a McNally hat to announce where he is headed. The room is stunned, because we are probably not the likely choice. I am out of my mind ecstatic, sitting in a hotel room in Orlando watching the scene. A few minutes later, Ahmad calls to tell me himself, followed by a congratulatory call from Coach Oliford. The next caller I can't understand because of all the screaming. Then I realize it is Cyndy. She makes things so much fun.

It has all come together. Now we need to win games and start planning for the future. This is exactly the home run I needed!

CHAPTER 15

THE COACH

Now that I have firmly established my credentials as a recruiter, I need to establish them just as securely as a coach. If I am going to be a successful head coach, I need to have significant experience and a solid track record so that a President or Athletic Director will have the confidence to hire me. I know what I have to do, and it is going to create some discomfort for a lot of people. But that is life. I know what I want and nothing will stop me from achieving my goals.

"You are doing a terrific job for us and you know I appreciate it," Coach Oliford begins. "I want to make sure you, Cyndy, and the baby are happy and comfortable here. I am going to give you a very substantial raise."

"I really appreciate that, Coach," I start, "but more important to me is increasing my coaching responsibilities and establishing myself as an excellent coach. I need to have people know that I am making decisions." "I get that and I'm sure we can do a lot of things to create those opportunities," Oliford continues. "I'm not talking about just working toward something, Coach. I want the title of co-offensive coordinator and I want to be very involved in the play calling," I respond. "Well, that would be difficult with

Pat already in place as the offensive coordinator, you know," he says. "It would create some very uncomfortable dynamics on the staff."

Here is what he doesn't know. I could care less what any of the other coaches think. Pat is an asshole and has treated me poorly from the start. From what I can see, most of the other guys are going nowhere. Making friends in this business is a myth. Driving toward my personal goals is reality. I have made my request and now we will find out just how bad Coach Oliford wants to win.

"Coach, I have already had ten job offers in the past two days, offering more money and any title I want. I'd like to stay here at McNally, but I have to be smart. I understand the staff dynamics that would be created, but I also understand winning and so do you. Players can make you a winner. Energy and creativity can make you a winner. I bring all these things to the staff. I realize this puts you in a tough spot, but to be honest, this is what I need to stay," I finish.

Now he actually has two choices. He either makes me the deal I want, or tells me "sorry, go get another job." There is a part of me that hopes he will tell me to "go to hell!" I would kind of respect that toughness. But, I believe we are going to be very good over the next few years. Being here to enjoy the victories and capitalize on them is best for me. I'm sure my dad, an unselfish high school coach, would be embarrassed at my selfishness and single-minded focus. I try not to think about that. The people who are mad will just have to get over it. I have my personal goals and they are No. 1 in my life.

"I will have to think about it for a day. This isn't what I was expecting from you and am disappointed in the position you are putting me in," he concludes. Oh please, how many other people's hamstrings did you slice to get to be a head coach? Spare me the disappointment B.S. This isn't personal, it's just business.

"Okay Coach, let me know," I say as I get up and leave his office.

For the first time, my first call is not to Cyndy. It is to my new agent, Jimmy Stallworth. He is my chief advisor now and the one who prepped me for the conversation with Oliford. Cyndy wouldn't like all this nasty stuff.

Jimmy answers his cell phone, "So how did it go?" "About like you would expect. He's pissed, but probably thinks he can't afford to lose me," I say. "Remember this," Jimmy says. "He's got his own multi-million-dollar deal to watch out for. He won't stand on principle or loyalty too long. Winning is a big payday for him and he needs you to help him win. I'll be shocked if he doesn't have this deal wrapped up in the morning."

"So, what are other schools saying?" I ask. "Three schools will make you the offensive coordinator and will beat anything McNally offers you financially. I just have to tell them if it's a go. You can't lose either way. But if we can do the McNally deal, it keeps you on a faster track, which is what we want."

I have now engaged in the gamesmanship that you have to play to get to the top. Jimmy is a big, loud, aggressive guy with a reputation for getting the job done. I picked him because he has a lot of big name college coaches as his clients. Every once in a while, I stop and think, "What am I doing? This is not the way I was raised." Then I refocus on where I want to go and everything else falls by the wayside. People are expendable, Jimmy keeps reminding me. I need to quit worrying about them. This is about me. I haven't even told Cyndy what I am doing. She is happy to have the baby and has made some great neighbor friends. The less she knows about all of this the better. It's not always in your best interest to involve too many people in your personal decision making because they can throw you off track. This is the first time I have made a major decision without input from Cyndy. It is another indication of how I have changed.

By the next morning, Jimmy has already leaked to the media that numerous schools are pursuing me. This is intended to put additional pressure on Oliford. Cyndy comes in carrying the morning paper and says, "Is this all true? You haven't said a word about this to me." I can tell she is pissed, but trying not to show it. "I didn't intend to bother you with this. I am trying to stay at McNally, so none of this may even matter," I say. "I just don't like not being in the know. It seems like you are now talking with your agent about these things rather than me," she says irritated.

"Jimmy is good and we need him to help us get to where we want to go. With the baby and all, I didn't want to burden you with job stuff. I'll let you know if anything gets serious. I met with Coach Oliford yesterday and asked for some different things. We'll see how he responds, but he had better not wait too long," I say smugly. "What did you ask him for, more money?" She asks.

"More money and the title of co-offensive coordinator. I want to be involved in all the play calling. I need that experience to get to be a head coach," I add. "I'm sure that went over big," Cyndy says. "Pat will hate that, and the others will be mad too. Congratulations, you just made me the most unpopular wife on the staff."

"We can't worry about that. We have to stay focused," I tell her. Cyndy leaves the room without saying another word. She doesn't have to. Maybe she doesn't really get it either, but I can't worry about that.

As I expected, Oliford agrees to my terms. He just wants a chance to talk to Pat first. "I think I owe the guy that much, and maybe I can try to make things as smooth as possible between you two," he says. "He's not going to be happy, I'm sure you know that."

"Thanks Coach, I won't let you down," I confirm. This is business. Time to move forward.

"You little prick," Click says as he enters my office. "You squeezed him into making you this deal for your own selfish reasons. I don't like anything about it and I'm not going to make this easy for you." At this point I have two choices, take the high road or go on the attack. I decide to attack.

"You're lucky I am here. You don't recruit. You sit your fat ass in this film room doing the same stuff you have done for ten years. We need some energy in the whole place. This change will probably make your career last longer," I respond. "I have forgotten more football than you know, kid. You need to be more respectful of people," Pat says.

"Well, this is the deal," I say, "so there is no sense arguing." And just to throw a little jab in to keep him off balance, "Don't worry, I don't want that donor's wife blowing me. She is all yours." With an incredulous look on his face, he storms out of my office. The battle has now officially begun.

I call Jimmy to let him know. He wants to leak the story before the university puts out some press release that confuses people. The story is my promotion, that is the lead, and we need to make sure it comes out that way. I know this will create further angst among the coaching staff. But, as Jimmy keeps reminding me, this is about me.

"So, I hear we are staying," Cyndy says. The irritation is clear in her voice. "Glad I could find out from Mary Jo (our neighbor). That wasn't embarrassing at all," she adds sarcastically. "I'm sorry. I meant to call you first thing, I just got side-tracked. You're happy though, right?" I try and soften the conversation.

"Of course, I am happy. What I am not happy about is somewhere along the line I lost my husband and replaced him with a football coach. That is not how we have been doing this," she finishes. "I'm very sorry. We'll talk about all this tonight and get everything back on track," I say. Of course, I have no intention of talking about this tonight. The deal is done and I need to get busy figuring out how to win games.

Stay focused on the goal of becoming a head coach, I repeat to myself over and over again.

CHAPTER 16

THE SEASON

As we head into the opening game, I have a lot of anxiety. It is mainly because I don't really trust what is going to happen because of the change in staff dynamics. However, I precipitated this realignment, so the media focus will be on me, and whether or not the change will be successful. In sports today, one game can be the final judgment of success or failure. You don't get time to establish the idea of building toward something. Expectations are high every week, for every game. This game, on top of everything else, is a nationally televised game against the California Golden Bears, Champions of the PAC-12 Conference last season. To make it tougher, we are playing the game at Cal.

This is going to be the first time we test our strategy for working together to call plays. Pat is still furious over the change and would like me to fail. But if we are unsuccessful, it will reflect on him as well. He has to try and make it work for his own self-preservation. I have tried my best to keep the players out of it, but he takes little shots all the time, just to try and keep the upper hand.

This is also the first time people will see Ahmad Burresh in a McNally University uniform, and the country is buzzing about his debut. I can tell Ahmad is excited as well. But, he is also feeling the pressure and I am trying to keep him calm. Pat Click will be in the press box. I am going to be on the sidelines signaling the plays. My presence on the sideline should help Ahmad, since he and I are so close. For me, this will be great national television exposure. I was sure I would have to fight to be on the field, but as it turned out, Pat has always been in the press box and likes it. He waddles his fat ass upstairs and eats hot dogs and drinks diet cokes in the air conditioning.

During warm-ups, I am coaching my guys but careful to keep an eye on Ahmad. I want him to succeed in his first game. He is a little high strung today and has dropped a few balls in warm ups. We have our first 15 plays already scripted, so the offensive guys know what needs to be done. In the first 15 plays, Ahmad won't get the ball right away. This gives him plenty of time to get into the flow of the game. Even for a great player, this is a big step up in competition.

We take the opening kickoff and return it to the 45-yard line. Our sideline erupts and Pat Click says into the headset, "Let's go for it and throw deep to Ahmad." I say, "Are you kidding me? The kid already feels enough pressure without changing the plan on the very first play." I really think he is just trying to mess with me on this. He knows better. "What's the point in having a superstar if you don't use him?" Pat says. "Okay, enough. I agree that we stick with the plan for the first few plays at least," Coach Oliford says into the headset. I tell our quarterback the play and we take the field.

In the first three plays, we get a first down. Play number four is a running play good for three yards. Here comes number five, going to the end zone to Ahmad. I am thinking to myself, "Here we go big man, show time!"

As our quarterback, Casey Cook, drops back, it all sets up perfectly. Ahmad gets a step on the cornerback and "Boom", touchdown for the freshman in his very first catch at McNally University. The hysteria reigns! As he heads back to the sidelines, he comes straight over to me. "Was that what you were looking for, Coach?" Ahmad says with a big smile on his face. I say, "Oh, I didn't see it. What happened?" We both hug as Coach Oliford walks over to me. "Way to hold your ground. Just keep doing the right things for this team. I have your back." I was hopeful that is how he felt, but it was nice to hear him say it. This is a guy who wants to win and that's all that matters.

As the game goes on, it is apparent we have a very good team. The addition of Ahmad has made us special. He finishes the game with 11 receptions for 181 yards, and three touchdowns. A star is born!

After the game, the locker room is electric. Everyone crowds around Coach Oliford to hear what he has to say. Everyone, except Pat Click, who has already headed to the coaches' locker room to shower and dress. What a selfish jerk. But I can't worry about that. This is exactly what this team needed, a big victory on the road against a very good team.

"I am really proud of you guys! Everyone contributed. We have great things ahead if we all stay focused, work hard, and remain unselfish," Coach Oliford tells the team. "Now who wants to lead us in the fight song?" The team jumps up and down as they loudly sing the school song.

The sports information director calls out the names of those to be interviewed in the press conference. I hear my name called. "What do they want with me?" I ask. "You called plays for the first time. The offense was spectacular, and you recruited Ahmad. What do you think they want to talk to you about?" Jim Simon says.

As I head to the interview room, I listen first to Coach Oliford comments to the press. He is very complimentary of me, and indicates that I have strengthened the offense and our play calling. That's all that matters, what he says about me publicly. Now I can be humble and deflect all the praise, which will make me seem like a good guy. It is the perfect set-up.

As we approach the rest of the season, I see a tremendous opportunity and find myself totally immersed in the job. At the same time, Cyndy and I are starting to drift further apart. She is busy with the baby and I have become more interested in being at the office, the greatest disease of any football coach.

When we land in Michigan after the Cal game, it is 3 a.m. I plan to head back to the office at 7 a.m., so I don't wake Cyndy. I leave her a note telling her I will call later and will be home around 10 p.m. I get busy and forget to call as the day goes along.

When I arrive home Sunday night, Cyndy is waiting for me and is not very happy. "I guess I should say congratulations on the game. I read all about you in the paper. Your folks called to see how you were doing. I told them I had not seen or talked to you. That was embarrassing, but I wasn't going to lie," she says. "I'm sorry, Baby. I just got so busy today. I'm doing this for us you know, and for our family. I have a chance to get a head coaching job out of all this. I have to stay focused," I respond.

"At the rate you are going, you may not have a family. And don't give me the whole "I'm doing it for us" stuff. This has become all about you. It used to be about us, but it doesn't seem like that now," Cyndy says.

She's right. I'm really not worried about anybody but me, but I can't afford to get bogged down in all of this. I need to strike while the iron is hot and these next few years will be critical.

"I promise I will be better. You are right and I love you," I say. We head back to the bedroom and Cyndy calms down. We actually spend some time together like the old days. This must be what they call "make-up sex"!

As the season progresses, we continue to get better and better. With a perfect record heading into the Ohio State game, we are one win away from the Rose Bowl. No one expected this. As we prepare for the game, I am continuing to get a lot of national publicity and our offense is producing big numbers. As a young coach, meeting with the ESPN announcers the week leading into the game raises your national profile. Once the announcers begin to talk about you on a national broadcast, others take notice and you start to be considered for head coaching jobs. This is all part of setting the stage.

I have also tried to make things better at home. Cyndy is too valuable an asset not to keep her at my side for the next phase of my career. She seems better, and is now already pregnant with a second child. She seems happy and that makes life a lot easier.

Coach Oliford is also happy. I think he realized things had gone stale with the team, particularly the offense. I have injected some new energy and focus that is paying off. The better we look, the better he looks, and he can parlay that into a better deal for himself as well.

Ohio State is really good. We know that, but we have a chance to do something special. Even if we lose, we will still end up in a big bowl game, even if it's not the Rose Bowl.

The game starts fast with us scoring first on an 80-yard drive. Ohio State answers back. We go back and forth with a halftime score of 14-14. But in the second half, the Buckeyes are simply too much for our defense and we end up losing 35-28. All in all, we made great progress and things look very promising for next season.

The team is positioned well. I am positioned well. Now we just need to make things happen.

CHAPTER 17

THE NEXT SEASON

The biggest difference between this season and last season is that our players expect to win and play in the Rose Bowl. I believe teams determine their own destiny and these kids have decided that they are going to be special. In this case, special means beating Ohio State and winning the Rose Bowl.

In fact, other than an early season loss at Florida, our season has been perfect. Winning the last regular season game against Ohio State has earned us a spot in the Rose Bowl. This will be the biggest spotlight for this football program in decades, and we seem to be embracing every minute of it. We came so close last season, but this year the quarterback is a year older and Ahmad Burresh has established himself as a Heisman Trophy candidate. It has been exciting, exhausting, and pressure filled as we keep winning games. Now we have the opportunity you dream about. We are going to play the big game on the big stage!

To make it even bigger, the opponent is USC, a fabled college football program, also with only one loss. This will be a big game for this program and a huge game for me.

"There is a lot of interest in you out there. Several schools are getting ready to pull the plug on their head coach. Some are still undecided. We need to try and get something done before the Rose Bowl, in case things don't go great," my agent Jimmy Stallworth tells me. "I know. I am getting ready for this game, recruiting, and keeping peace at home," I respond. With the baby, Cyndy is worn out. I am not there much and she feels pressure as well. She also knows the likelihood is that we are moving somewhere again. Don't get me wrong, she wants to be a head coach's wife and she grew up with money. She can't wait to build a big house, hire someone to help with the baby, and start living a higher lifestyle. Right now, life is stressful!

"Well, let me tell you what you better do. You better get ready for some interviews because this is your big chance. You never know when you will get it again," Jimmy reminds me. "Stop worrying about McNally, that's Oliford's job. You worry about yourself. Remember, without you, he's not playing in the Rose Bowl. No offense to anyone, but I don't give a shit about the place and neither should you. This is about money. Nothing else matters, get it?"

"I know. It's just a lot coming at once and we don't even know which schools have an opening yet," I say. "That will take care of itself. Just get your head right," Jimmy finishes.

I head home to talk with Cyndy about all of this. "You realize you might have to go along on an interview, and certainly for a press conference, if something happens." I say. "I know. My mom is set to fly up here if we need her. I know the drill," she says. Cyndy understands this business better than anyone I know. Even though we have drifted a little, this is what makes her a champ. It's really more of a partnership, both focused solely on the prize ahead. Now we are actually nearing the goal. We head to bed not knowing what the next day might bring.

I wake up early and turn on ESPN to see a report that Florida A&I is going to fire their coach. In my opinion, that is one of the top ten jobs in the country and a place where I can win big. It's also in the heart of the best recruiting state in the country, Florida.

I wake up Cyndy. "Florida A&I is open. I want that job," I say very directly. "You think you will have a chance? Won't they try and hire a sitting head coach?" Cyndy asks. "Probably. But the place needs energy, life, and someone who can recruit his ass off. I'm the perfect candidate," I say.

I pick up the phone and call Jimmy. "If you are worth a shit, you'll get me the Florida A&I job," I say. Jimmy laughs. "I talked to the president and the athletic director last night. They are very interested. They just have to take a shot at a couple of big names to keep the alumni off their asses. My guess is they won't get one of those guys. Then we will have a chance." That is why I hired him. He is very good and very connected. He has already put the wheels in motion, so I have to go to work and draw up a plan for Florida A&I. It is all very exciting and energizing.

I turn to Cyndy and say, "we have a chance, so that is really all we can ask for." She hugs me and says, "We are ready to go whenever you need us. We believe in you and are excited for us!"

It's hard to keep my mind on something when I really want something else. However, I need to stay focused on getting ready for the Rose Bowl. If I do get the job, all eyes in Florida will be on me to see how we do in that game. I need to be at the top of my game in every respect.

The media hype begins and as expected, the Florida A&I people float out some big names as possible candidates. Other names are mentioned, mine being one. That will create a little distraction here, but I will play it very low key.

Coach Oliford walks into my office and closes the door. "Have you got a chance at the Florida A&I job?" "I really don't know, Coach. I haven't heard anything from them, but I do think it is a great job," I respond. "It is a great job. Just promise me you'll keep me in the loop on all of this. I understand what you want, but we need to win the Rose Bowl," he adds. "No one wants to win the Rose Bowl more than me, Coach, trust me. You will get my best game yet, no matter what the situation is," I say. "Great. And another thing. Don't take a bad job. You are a good coach. Wait for a job like Florida A&I. That's just my advice," he adds. "I appreciate it, Coach, and for your confidence in me. Let's go beat the Trojans!"

Three days later, Jimmy calls. "The Florida folks are going to fly up to Detroit tomorrow for an initial meeting. They will fly into a private hangar at Atlantic Aviation and meet you in a conference room there. No one can know about this meeting. You can't even tell Oliford. The meeting is at 9 p.m. so no one will even know you are gone," he says.

Wow, this thing is real. I am getting the interview I want at a big-time place. I know I promised to keep Coach Oliford in the loop, but what the heck. He doesn't tell me everything he does!

I hang up the phone and call Cyndy, who is very excited. It's nice to have her to talk to about all of this. "Let's get you ready for tomorrow night," she says. "Better hurry home."

I wake up at 5:30 a.m. the next day, completely energized and focused on this initial interview. I do have practice today and recruits to call, but my mind will be on Florida A&I. The trick will be not letting others know about the meeting or the interest they have in me. 9 p.m. seems like an eternity.

As I walk into the Atlantic Aviation waiting area, I am quickly greeted by a man I recognize as Curt Feeny, the Florida A&I Athletic Director. He whisks me off into a private meeting room before anyone can see me.

"Sorry for the quick handshake, but we are trying not to let anyone know we are here, or that you are here," Feeny says as he opens the door to the conference room. "Meet our President Guy Twillie, and two of our biggest donors, Ken Wilson and Ted Morgan." I shake hands all around and try to make some brief connection with each person. I think it is important to create some warmth with each individual right away. This is really just recruiting at a much higher level.

The athletic director is leading the interview, but it is clear the other three will likely have the ultimate authority. I never really like the idea of boosters sitting in on the interview, but clearly these guys have a big say in what happens, so I need to connect with them as well.

"I am honored to be here and excited for the chance to talk with you about this job. Florida A&I is a great University and exactly the kind of place where I know you can not only win championships, but sustain a great program year after year. You have great leadership, great support, great facilities, every ingredient needed to succeed," I start off.

"We happen to agree with your initial thoughts," President Twillie says. "Why do you think you are ready for this job? It's a big step." This is the big question of course, and I have been preparing for this exact question. I start talking and laying out my plan in detail.

The meeting goes on for almost three hours until midnight. I can tell they are not only engaged, but enthused. They have been trying to hire big name guys who they have probably either had to recruit or beg. Now they are sitting with a guy who is recruiting them. The natural instinct is to feel better about me. I'm convinced it went well enough to get a second interview. Let's hope I am right!

As I leave, we all shake hands and AD Feeny says to me, "I will call you in the morning to talk further and see what you think." That has to be a good sign.

As I drive home it all begins to sink in. At a very young age, I have a chance to get "The Job" I have wanted and have been working toward since I started coaching. It is like a dream.

My attention slips back to the business at hand. We need to win the Rose Bowl regardless. I change my plans and turn left, heading back to the office. There is a lot of preparation to do for this game and I have been distracted.

I call Cyndy to tell her everything went well and I am headed to the office. She understands that there are too many big things happening to get any rest. Sleep can wait until after the Rose Bowl.

As I walk into the building, I notice that Coach Oliford's car is in the parking lot and his office light is partially on. As I walk by his office, it is pretty clear he is in there and I hear the giggles of a young woman. I guess he is enjoying the results of going to the Rose Bowl as well. I'm equally sure his wife thinks he is on the road recruiting players, not on top of a 27-year old.

I can't worry about that. I've got my own opportunities at hand and I cannot afford to screw this up.

CHAPTER 18

DREAM JOB

At 8 a.m. the next morning my cell phone rings. It is Curt Feeny calling. "We really enjoyed the conversation last night. In fact, all of us were pretty pumped up on the plane flight home," he says.

"I really enjoyed it as well and it was a pleasure to meet all of you," I respond.

"Sorry for the late night, but it seemed like the conversation was such that it was easy to let the time get away. We didn't land here in Tampa until 2:30 a.m." Curt adds.

"That wasn't a problem at all. In fact, I came back to the office to get ready for Rose Bowl practices, so I haven't been to bed," I counter, knowing full well this will impress him and reinforce the work ethic portion of our conversation. I can just see him calling the other three and telling them I went back to the office after our meeting. These kinds of guys love this stuff. If you are a football coach, the smartest thing you can do is keep throwing out these stories about the long hours and crazy lifestyle. It creates kind of an urban legend among fans and boosters. The reality is a lot of people work hard. Coaches are just the ones who talk about it all the time. Hey, give them what they want, I say!

"What we would like to do is fly you and your wife down here for 24 hours, very confidentially, to see the campus and talk further. Is there a time that would work in the next day or so?" Curt asks.

"Absolutely, the sooner the better from my standpoint. I will have to tell Coach Oliford what is going on. We can tell the rest of the coaches that I am out recruiting," I add. "That's fine. Can we target picking you up tonight about 6 p.m. and returning tomorrow night?" "I'm sure that is fine. I just need to let Cyndy know and make arrangements for our daughter. I'm sure we can work it all out. Give me an hour, and I will call you back," I say.

"Great. I will look forward to spending more time together," Curt adds. "Me too," I say enthusiastically.

I immediately call Cyndy to tell her what is going on. Like a trooper, she is not only excited but immediately says, "I will solve the situation with the baby. I can have Mom on a flight up here this afternoon. She is expecting it. You don't worry about that."

I am a selfish person. Cyndy is not. She just solves problems, keeps the pressure off me, and makes things so much easier. She is a lot of the reason I have been able to rise quickly in this business. I am very lucky!

"You are the greatest," I say. "If you need to buy something new to wear or whatever, just do it. Also, pack for another couple of days. I have a feeling if this goes well we might just stay down there for a press conference." It sounds arrogant, but I know how these things go, and if they want me back down there in 24 hours, they are serious. I believe in planning for success, not failure. I believe in creating opportunities and driving them to the finish line.

The next task is to tell Coach Oliford what is going on. I'm sure he will be supportive. It makes him look good. It's also not to his advantage to have it leak out, in case I don't get the job. It could make our program look weak and lose some credibility with the fans.

I knock on his office door. He looks exhausted and I know why. "Have you got a second, Coach?" "Sure. Come on in. I'm guessing you have a chance at the Florida A&I job," he says.

From there, I proceed to tell him everything and apologize for not telling him about the first interview. I say it would have cost me the job. He is cool about all this and happy for me. He just asks one question that I am expecting. "Will you stay through the Rose Bowl game if you get the job?"

"Coach, after the interview last night I came back to the office to prepare for the Rose Bowl. No matter what happens, I am going to stay and help us beat USC," I say firmly. "That's all I need to hear. Good luck," he adds.

With that over, I head home to pack so we are ready to leave immediately after practice. Being on the field today will keep my mind occupied while I wait for the trip to Tampa.

As we exit the private jet, I see both Curt Feeny and his wife waiting for us inside the private hangar. They greet me warmly and I introduce them to Cyndy. As we climb into the black Mercedes, it feels like an out of body experience. A young kid from a tiny town in Ohio is now being vetted for the head football coaching job at one of the top schools in the country. To get here, you have to do a good job, but you also have to be lucky. I have had all of the pieces fall into place.

"Cyndy, we are really happy that you could come along, especially on such short notice," Curt says. "My mom jumped on a flight at noon from Birmingham and she is staying with our daughter so it worked out great. I wouldn't miss this for the world. I have already heard so many great things about you and the university," she adds. She is always the consummate recruiter. She has the ability to hit all the right notes.

"We are having dinner at the President's Mansion. Attending the dinner will be all the men you met the other night and their wives. You are actually going to be staying with the President and his wife at the Mansion. This way your visit can remain very confidential," Curt tells us. With that we speed off, headed on a short tour through the city. Everything feels real to me now and I am trying hard to keep my emotions in check. I don't want to appear too "amped up" and not mature enough for the job, but believe me, I am "amped up."

The President's Mansion is impressive. It once belonged to a wealthy banking family in Tampa who eventually donated it to the University. Now it is the center of activities hosted by President Twillie and his wife, Fern. As we step out of the car, they are both there to greet us. In these types of situations, I am smart enough to let Cyndy take over. Unlike me, she grew up in this type of setting and is perfectly at home. Before the night is over, the entire group will be infatuated with her. We head into the house, and I once again meet Ken Wilson and Ted Morgan. We are introduced to their wives, both of whom must be 30 years younger than their husbands. Coaches aren't the only ones attracted to money!

It's clear the evening is really just social, probably to make sure they like us and we fit into settings like this. The biggest difference from being an assistant coach to a head coach is that you have to assume the mantle of the position. In this state, being the football coach is a big deal and these guys want to make sure I can meet Trustees, raise money from major donors, and even be an asset with the state legislators. There is a lot more to the job than running the team and calling the plays. This is what tonight is all about, their assessment of whether or not I can do all of that. I need to be at my best socially and allow Cyndy to work her magic!

"So, Coach," (that's a good sign when they start to call you Coach. They are moving you into a position of prominence in their world). "What do you think we need to do to get this program to the National Championship?" Ken Wilson asks. There it is, the standard at Florida A&I. It is not a certain number of wins or a conference championship. They want to win a National

Championship to consider the program successful. Interestingly, they have never won one.

"Recruit," I answer very simply. "The biggest mistake a coach can make is thinking it is him, or his scheme, that will create success. Don't get me wrong. We will coach them better than anyone. Players make coaches great, and we ought to be able to recruit every player we want to this university."

I can tell right away that I have hit the right tone with the group. They are not looking for an egomaniac who thinks he is the next Vince Lombardi. No one is. A coach who is grounded in reality has a big edge over the others. I find more and more that coaches want everyone to believe they are the reason for winning. I also know that every President wants a more holistic sales pitch.

"We will not only recruit, but we will recruit top quality people who will bring honor, not embarrassment, to the University. President Twillie, you should never have to answer questions about the failures of our team or players. My job is to keep that off your plate," I add. I can see he is pleased with that comment, and Fern is particularly pleased.

"Let's head into the dining room to enjoy dinner," President Twillie says. "We can continue the conversation in there."

The rest of the evening goes very well. Cyndy steals the show, and everyone departs in high spirits feeling like we are headed in the right direction. At least it seems that way to me. As we head to the guest quarters in the Mansion, the President pulls me aside and says, "I am hopeful this will all work out. You seem like the kind of person who will have great success here. I just hope if we get to that point where we are moving toward a deal, some agent doesn't get over zealous. Remember, we are taking a certain amount of risk, and will likely get some criticism, for not hiring a sitting head coach. I am fine with that, but everyone needs to remain realistic about where things stand." In a very dignified way, he just told me that the only person who can screw this up now is a greedy agent. The message is heard loud and clear.

"I appreciate your advice, and I am grateful for this opportunity. All I would ever ask from you in all of our dealings is to be treated fairly," I respond.

"Fair enough. It is great to have you here tonight. I will see you down here tomorrow at 8 a.m. Good night," Twillie adds.

I fill Cyndy in on the last conversation as we get ready for bed. "He's right, you know. Win and then you can be a jerk in the next negotiations," she says laughing.

Rather than try and talk on the phone, I text my agent the basics of the conversation. His response is simple and direct. "Don't worry, I won't screw this up and you will still get paid. That's why you hired me."

It's true. A good agent can easily pay for himself. Jimmy Stallworth is considered the best and people seem to like him. I just need to get the job and I am confident he will handle the rest.

The next morning is designed to quietly see the facilities and spend time with the athletic director. He and I have hit it off well, and these will be the first real discussions of substance. This is often where deals get a little dicey. In my case, I want the job so I will say anything he wants to hear. Once I get the job, there is not much he can do if I head off in another direction. The reality is the job of an athletic director is a no-win situation. He puts his faith in the guy he hires and no matter how the coach acts, the two have to work together. Fans will blame the athletics director for all coaching failures, and conversely give him no credit for the success of the coach. I'm certain Feeny understands this, so he is probably most interested in trying to figure me out. I need to try and calm any apprehensions he might have about me right from the start.

"You have a lot of experience and this would be my first head coaching job. I will need to lean on you for a lot of advice as we get this program headed toward a championship," I begin. I can immediately see that he is pleased with this approach.

"I will do anything I can, within reason, to help you succeed, if you are our coach. It is in everyone's best interests to work shoulder to shoulder to drive this program forward. It is important that our donors and fans see this as well. They don't like discord," he tells me.

From there we have a very in depth talk about the program. It is a good session and he seems to feel very comfortable.

As we conclude, he says, "we are all on board with you becoming the head coach at Florida A&I. We just need to see if we can reach an agreement."

"I'm sure we can. My agent, Jimmy Stallworth, is waiting to get the call that we are ready to proceed. I just need to let him know," I respond. "And Curt, thank you for this opportunity. You won't be sorry."

With that, I call Jimmy, who lives in Atlanta, and he is on the next flight to Tampa. He lands around 2 p.m.

"If you can, I'd like to have you stay here and see if we can pull a deal together quickly. If we can, we will have a press conference tomorrow morning," he adds. "I have one request. My mother-in-law is with our daughter right now. Can we get them down here for the press conference? It just wouldn't seem right not to have our daughter with us. My folks are right in Ohio. They could drive over to Michigan and come up with Cyndy's mom and the baby. My dad is a high school coach. I think it is important to have the entire family if possible," I ask.

Feeny smiles and says, "Family is always first around here. If we get a deal, I will have Ken Wilson get them in his plane." And so, it all begins.

I head back to the hotel where they have moved us, and wait for Cyndy while the negotiations begin. I have never been through this, but I know how it works. Jimmy and I have already talked about what I want. Now he becomes the hard ass battling on my behalf. He will insist that I know nothing about the details of the negotiations, I am just concerned about coaching. His job is to get the deal we want and leave no hard feelings. If there is angst, it is toward him, not me. Everything he will request comes directly from me, but the secret is to make the athletic director and President think it is all the agent. You hear administrators say all the time, "I like our coach, but his agent was a bear to deal with." That is exactly how we want to be perceived.

The biggest sticking point for me is the guaranteed money. Years on a contract mean nothing and won't stop them from firing you. The only thing that is guaranteed is the money. So, the bigger the guarantee, the better the protection. I am focused on getting big guaranteed money in this first contract. The rest is less important to me.

Jimmy calls me when he lands and is heading to meet Feeny and their lawyers. "How hard do you want me to push?" He asks. "Just don't lose the deal, Jimmy. I want this job and when we win, I'll let you crush them." We both laugh.

Cyndy arrives back at the hotel after some confidential house hunting. It is a strange feeling, sitting in a hotel room, waiting for a deal to come together. There is tremendous anxiety, but honestly, at this point neither side is likely to back away from the deal. It's just a dance now.

My phone rings and I see it is my dad calling. It is an unusual time of day for him to be calling. "Hi Dad, what's up?" I ask hoping everything is okay. "The whole town is buzzing. ESPN is reporting that you are going to be the head coach at Florida A&I. Is that true?" he asks. I am stunned. I had no idea this was leaking out, but it could not have come from my end. I have not even told my parents. Cyndy's folks know, but you can trust them to keep a secret. It's either coming from Coach Oliford, which I doubt, or from the Florida people. My guess is some of the boosters down here are getting ahead of themselves.

"Dad, you have to keep this very confidential. We are down here right now but it is not a done deal. They have asked me not to tell a soul, but I will keep you posted. If people ask, just saying "if that were true, I would probably know about it and I haven't heard anything from my son."

"Of course, son. This is exciting and it would be a great job," he says. "Dad, if it all comes together, we are working on arrangements to get you and Mom down here tomorrow for a press conference. Can you get free if that happens?" "You bet. Just keep me posted. I love you and am proud of you," he finishes.

Now I feel like a jerk. Here is my dad, a coach, a smart man, and I haven't made him a part of any of this. I have been so wrapped up in myself I have forgotten to think about my parents. They are great and always so forgiving, but I wonder what they really think? Like many times before, I vow to myself to do better in the future.

At the same time, Cyndy is on the phone with her dad giving him the same instruction.

"Did you see the ESPN report?" Jimmy says when I pick up the phone. "They are pretty wound up here about it. I told them it didn't come from us. I think they know that but they are worried about the President getting pissed because he has not told his Board of Trustees."

"The best part is that all the guys on ESPN and other shows are talking about what a great hire it is. Everyone around here is getting excited. You know what that means? More leverage to get the deal closed on our terms," Jimmy add. "I'll keep you posted."

All of the sudden I realize, Jimmy created all of this publicity to get us a better deal. That includes getting the guys on TV to say it is a great hire.

"Now I understand why we hired Jimmy," I say to Cyndy. From there I fill her in on the game he is playing.

About 5 p.m. Jimmy calls back. "The deal is done. There will be a press conference tomorrow at 1 p.m. They want to sign it and announce it by press release at 9 p.m. tonight. Their attorneys are typing right now. Let me tell you, it is a hell of a deal. Six years and more money than you can ever spend. Congratulations!" "Thanks Jimmy, you are the best," I say as I hang up.

As Cyndy runs over to hug me, it is no longer a dream. The dream job is now my reality!

CHAPTER 19

PRESS CONFERENCE

"You will knock them dead. Just be yourself and they will love you. Don't forget to introduce our parents," Cyndy reminds me. She is my biggest fan and best advisor.

I have heard the notion that you have to "win the press conference." That might work for the first eight months or so, but then you have to win games. For me, the press conference today is about connecting with our current players and building excitement with future recruits. The fans will be excited, but they are not my primary audience.

After the usual nonsense where the athletic director insists that I was their first choice and the right person to lead the program into the future, I take the stage for the obligatory photo with the school ball cap on. Then I take the podium for my first introduction.

"Just a few minutes ago, I met with the most important group of men in this process, our current team. They are a terrific group of young men and a coaching change can be difficult for them, but it can also be exciting. I will tell you what I told them. Today we hit the re-set button. This is a new beginning for everyone. This program has won in the past, but that is the past. We are going to live in the future and that means focusing on the current players and those we are recruiting to join them. If you want to be a part of something special, get to Tampa as soon as you can. You will be in for a heck of a ride."

"Before I go on, you need to meet the best recruiter on our staff, my wife Cyndy, with our daughter Katie. Cyndy is the greatest partner a coach could ever have, and she is a fabulous wife and mother. So good, in fact, she is ready to be a mom again." Everyone in the room laughs as she stands up and waves. She is radiant and people are immediately taken with her.

"Also, meet the four most important people in our lives, our parents. We were both fortunate to be raised by wonderful people who taught us the right set of values. My dad was my first football coach and is still my hero. I hope I can make an impact on young men the way he has been able to. I had the single greatest mom growing up. She made our home so happy. I hope we will be able to duplicate that type of family atmosphere here at Florida A&I for every one of our players. I am confident we can."

"The one thing I did tell our players is that I am going to coach the Rose Bowl game for McNally University. It is an important game and I don't want to be unfair to the players there. They worked hard to earn this opportunity. What I hope it reinforces with our players at FAI is the manner in which I treat my players. Coaching the Rose Bowl game is the right thing to do and I believe our current players will appreciate the commitment. It was the one thing Coach Oliford asked, and I owe him a great deal. The next month will be wild, but also the most exciting of my entire life."

At this point, I take questions from the reporters. They ask questions about offense, defense, coaching staff, etc. It all feels good and seems natural to me.

"Great job. Everyone loved you and the response from our current players was excellent. We are off to a great start," an ecstatic Curt Feeny says. When everyone likes the coach, the pressure on the athletic director is dramatically reduced. Today, Curt got his man and the Florida A&I nation is excited. Now we have to get to work.

CHAPTER 20

BALANCING ACT

As we fly back to Michigan, I start to map out how I will manage two very demanding jobs for the next month. These things always sound great when you first agree to them, but coaching the bowl game is a big commitment. Reality sets in as I note what needs to be done. On top of that, I have to hire an entire coaching staff because I am not currently a head coach bringing a staff along with me.

The first thing I need is a great director of football operations. This guy will help me pull everything together and make the transition much easier. The person I hire will move to Tampa right away and begin work on the ground. This will be a key ingredient to getting everything moving. I have a guy in mind who I have gotten to know over the years. He is the director of football operations at Indiana, so this would be a great step up for him both in terms of pay and prestige. His name is Cal Smith, and he will be my first call after we land.

When we touch down at the airport, I kiss Cyndy, Katie, and my parents goodbye, and head to the office. This is the beginning of a wild month.

With a few exceptions, all of the guys on the McNally staff are genuinely happy for me. Coach Oliford is great and appreciative that I kept my word to coach the bowl game. Most of the assistants have some friend they want me to hire, but then always throw in "and if you pay me enough, maybe I'd go along." What they don't know is that I would have very little interest in many of them. They don't work hard enough in recruiting.

As you would expect, Pat Click is a complete jerk. "So why did you come back? We can handle the Rose Bowl without you. In fact, it would be better because we could get back to the way it used to be around here. You just came in here for a few years so you could get yourself a head coaching job. Don't act like you are doing us any favors," he says.

"Pat, I came back for our players and because Coach asked me to. That's it. Yes, you can go back to the way it used to be, watching someone else play in the Rose Bowl." I just couldn't resist the dig. I wouldn't normally do that, but I am sick of this guy and we will never be friends. With that, I head back to my office to call Cal Smith.

Like the professional he is, Cal answers the phone instantly with, "Congratulations! You will do a fantastic job at Florida A&I." "Only if you are willing to do it along with me," I respond. "Here's the deal, $50,000 more than you are making and I will get you an associate athletic director title." With that, the deal is done and Cal is ready to head to Tampa tomorrow to get started.

My next call is to Curt Feeny. "I got a fantastic guy to come as director of football operations. His name is Cal Smith and he is at Indiana. I told him we would pay him $200,000 and make him an associate AD. Can you have someone call him and make flight arrangements to get him in there tomorrow?" I add. "Hang on just a second," Curt says. "We can't just hire people quite like that. We have some human resources stuff we have to go through first. That is also a lot more than I was planning on paying for that position." Here we go. I guess I am going to have to set the tone right off the bat. "Curt, I get all that, but you hired me to run the program and win. That means getting the best people. That won't happen unless we can clear the decks and keep all this moving. I have complete confidence you can get all of this done for me. You will love Cal. Trust me on this," I add.

"Okay," Curt says reluctantly, "I will get this handled, but please keep me in the loop and try and give me some breathing room on campus." I try and bring his spirits back up a little. "We are going to hire a great staff, and you are going to be a hero. Mark that down, Curt."

I have been thinking about possible assistants for some time now, so I pretty much have a target list. My formula is going to be fairly simple. I will hire a great offensive and defensive coordinator, and then seven assistant coaches who can recruit. That is how we are going to win, with better players than everyone else. Coaching is very important, but great players are the key.

I start down the list to make some initial calls to potential assistants. I am confident I will have good success hiring assistants, for these reasons. Coaches will see this as a chance to coach at a great place, work for a new head coach with a long-term deal, and if we have success, create their own opportunities. There is something exciting about being at the beginning of a journey where everyone is on the same page.

I will hire one coach from McNally, Carl Samuels. From the moment we met him at the airport in Detroit, he has continued to impress both Cyndy and me more every day.

I want to hire Nick Sallee, the offensive coordinator at Auburn. He has done a great job, but they are always second fiddle to Alabama. I figure he might be ready for a change. They also run an offense similar to what I am doing at McNally, so the transition would be easy. After a long conversation, Nick says he thinks he is in, but wants to sleep on it. My sense is he will want to come, plus I just agreed to make him one of the highest paid coordinators in the country. Money is still always the key factor.

Michigan has a defensive coordinator who gives us headaches every year. If I can hire him, it would be a real coup. His name is Bucky Fox and he is just as wild as his name. Kids love to play for him and he brings energy and passion to defense. When I call him, he seems very surprised. "The way you beat our butts this year, I'm surprised you would have any interest in me coming to Florida with you," he says. I start recruiting. "There is nobody harder to prepare for than you. I love your schemes, your adjustments, and in Conference America, you can make all the difference. Name your salary and let's get this done." "Let me think about it, but I am interested," Bucky replies. This means I have a reasonable chance. I just have to keep recruiting him and hope Michigan won't match the salary.

The six other coaches I already know pretty well from recruiting against them. I will start calling them over the next few days, but I want to get the coordinators hired first to make a big splash right out of the gate. The other assistants won't have the same sizzle, but let me tell you, they will be able to recruit and our players will love them.

This is where the time crunch hits me. I look at my watch and I have to meet with my current players in 15 minutes. Since I knew this was a possibility, I have already drawn up all the meeting and practice plans for the entire Rose Bowl preparation. I knew if I got the job, it would be hard to find the time. Now I am really glad I did.

The players are great when they come into the meeting. Each one hugs me and seems excited for me. I know they appreciate that I am going to coach the bowl game. I have been very upfront with them so they are neither surprised nor mad. They knew I wanted to be a head coach.

"I'm glad they didn't call any of you guys to check on me," I start out to lighten the mood. "I am focused on beating USC and having a great time together in Pasadena. Then we can all celebrate afterwards. I love you guys and I'm glad we have one more game together."

James Gardner stand up and says, "Coach, we all came here to play for you. You have been real with us and we love you. We are going to give you everything we've got until the last play of the bowl game." It doesn't get any better than that. We all hug and head to the practice field.

It is nice to get back out on the practice field, but once you have taken another job, you have moved on mentally. Practice is like an out of body experience where I am doing the things I am supposed to do, but my mind is in a distant place. That's the way it is going to be through the game, physically here and mentally there. That's why I need Cal in Tampa, to take all of the things going on in my mind and put them into action at Florida A&I. The list will be long and continuous, but he will make it all happen.

That night when I head home, it is great to walk into a calm environment and have Cyndy and our daughter Katie greet me. After a nice dinner, I get the first good night's sleep I have had in a week. Funny thing is, it will probably be the last good night's sleep in a long time.

An interesting thing happens to you when you decide to coach college football. You discover that sleep is a luxury. It starts when you are a graduate assistant, often working through the night to break down film for the assistant coaches to use the next day. Sleeplessness seems to continue the rest of your career.

The next morning starts with a welcome call from Nick Sallee, saying he is in. Perfect. Now I need to recruit Bucky a little more and we will be off to a great start. It will help lure Bucky when he hears that Nick has accepted the job. Most guys want to be on a staff with other excellent coaches. I pick up the cell phone and dial

Bucky. He takes my call which is always a good sign. "I had a hard time sleeping last night hoping you would take the D coordinator job, Bucky," I start. "This would be a hard place to leave. They treat me great here at Michigan," he responds. "I'm sure they do Bucky, and they should. But I think we can do something special at Florida A&I and I want you to be a part of that, a big part. That is why I would make you assistant head coach," I add. I go on to tell him about Nick, Cal, and all the good things that are already in place. By the end of the call, he has all but said yes. "I will call you back before the end of the day," he says. "Great. Let's get this thing going," I exclaim. He would have said yes, but he must have told Michigan he wouldn't say yes until he talked to them again. I don't think we would be this far unless he really wanted to come to Tampa.

I give Cyndy a quick update. She is excited. I ask her to call Nick Sallee's wife to tell her how thrilled we all are they are joining the staff. As I leave the house, I call Cal to tell him about Nick and ask him to send flowers to Nick's wife so she knows how fired up we are.

Now it is time to start hiring the rest of the staff. I am not concerned because I have a good list, many of whom can head to Tampa right away and get out recruiting for us. There isn't much recruiting time in December, but we want to take advantage of the time we get. One by one, coaches start to say yes and I am energized just talking to them. This will not only be a great staff, but fun people to be around. By the end of the day, Bucky has called to say he is coming and I have hired most of the rest of the staff. We have officially started the process of building Florida A&I.

After each success in the coaching hiring, I have to switch gears and go back to coaching for the Rose Bowl. I am somewhat "going through the motions," yet when I get on the field with the players, that becomes the best part of the day. That is the reason I decided to get into coaching in the first place.

By the next morning, I will begin a routine that will continue until I eventually land on the ground in Tampa. At 6:00 a.m. each day, I have a conference call with our new staff at Florida A&I. The purpose is to keep the program moving and to discuss recruiting. Each morning, they give me a list of recruits to call that night when the Bowl game obligations are finished for the day. It's not ideal, but it is all part of the process of putting a program together in my own mold.

The coach before me at Florida A&I had pretty much retired on the job. The team was generally undisciplined and sloppy on the field and had a ridiculous number of players in trouble off the field. The previous coach had spent most of his career in the NFL, failing miserably as a head coach, twice. He hoped that his return to his alma mater would be different, but no such luck. His personal life got in the way of his professional life. He drank nearly every night with his best friend and former teammate. It was not uncommon for him to show up at team functions drunk. The public never knew all of this, but the university had no choice but to fire him. The players saw his behavior as acceptable, justifying their own bad behavior. Players view coaches as role models, good or bad. Obviously, we have a lot of cleaning up to do.

This is a new day, however, and we will need to be focused and disciplined from the beginning. We will break these bad habits and build perfection. The new day begins today!

CHAPTER 21

LEARN HOW TO FINISH

One of the things we always remind our players is to finish. This applies to everything you do. Now I find myself having to do the exact same thing as I complete my obligations at McNally University. It is an odd time for me. Here I am, sitting at a major press conference talking about how I am going to attack the USC defense on Monday and praising players I am going to be leaving behind. In addition, I am managing some very awkward staff dynamics for the remainder of the bowl trip. This entire time, Florida A&I is on my mind. It teaches me grit and determination. I have to figure out how to stay focused on what I am doing now, but when I have breaks, I focus on where I am heading.

But first, I have to finish!

As I kiss Cyndy goodbye to board the team bus for the Rose Bowl game, I have the overwhelming feeling that things will never be the same again. When the game is over, Cyndy and Katie will fly back to Michigan with the rest of the team. Florida A&I has sent a jet to Pasadena to take me back to Tampa at the end of the game. Of course, the plane is filled with top boosters who want to see in person what they are paying for. I don't mind, it is just the beginning of what will be a life that is really not my own. Once you become a head coach, it seems like you are never alone in a room. There is always someone who needs or wants something. It is hard for that not to take a toll on your marriage. I wonder at what point it changed for Coach Oliford. Here we are at the Rose Bowl game, and I have seen at least two beautiful young women that I have seen around him before. It's almost like his wife knows it and has chosen to turn her head. And he has gotten pretty brazen to have both of them at the bowl game! Who knows what the repercussions will be if one finds out about the other?

But this is college football, and nailing the head coach is a prize, no matter how old or unappealing he might be. Some young women grow up worshipping football coaches and players. They may have some weird psychological issue about craving the approval of their dad, who knows. Whatever the case, the dysfunction is alive and well right in our midst. For me, I just want to win the game and get on the plane out of here!

There is nothing quite as exhilarating as pulling up to the stadium in the team bus for a big game. You hear people refer to the electricity. That is probably the best term for it. If you love the game and are a competitive person, you are really "fired up" by the time you get to the stadium. This sensation carries you through the rest of the day. Thousands of people line the street leading into the Rose Bowl, your fans cheering you, the opponent's fans baiting you. I still can't quite come to grips with 50-year old people flipping me "the bird", but it happens over and over again.

Once inside the gates of the Rose Bowl, we unload the buses and head to the locker room. Everyone has a routine they go through in the locker room before games. Today, I alter my usual routine and walk throughout the entire locker room and speak to every player. I have either coached or recruited a high percentage of these guys. It will be tough to see them all after the game, so I try and do it now. I end up spending more time with some of the kids than others. It gets emotional. They will move on quickly to a new coach, and I have an entire new team waiting for me in Florida. But still, this is final!

With some players, it is just a hug. With others, it's talking about the fun we have had and the excitement of today. For others, like Ahmad Burresh, it's very emotional because he is like part of our family. With these kind of exchanges, we play it down and talk about how we will still see each other all the time and talk by phone regularly. That's all well intentioned, but will be limited by distance to a large extent. It doesn't make it any easier though, and we all agree today will be our best day together yet.

As I head to the coaches' locker room to get dressed, it is a funny feeling to be pulling on the McNally colors for the last time. That emotion all changes when I see Pat Click's fat ass sitting in the locker room. His smug look tells me he is obviously happy I am leaving. It's good though. It snaps me back to reality and the need to focus on winning this particular game.

The ESPN cameras will likely show me often and talk about my new position at Florida A&I. In reality, I am playing to two fans bases. McNally fans hoping to win and Florida A&I fans hoping I can coach! For me, I'm coaching only for our current players and for future recruits I hope to sign at Florida A&I. Never forget that players win games and make you a good coach. Today is about winning, and making an impression for the future.

The game starts just as expected with both teams trying to get established in a highly-charged atmosphere. I would like to be a little more wide-open on offense, but Coach Oliford doesn't want us to get too fancy on the first series. After we exchange punts, I suggest we go for it with a deep pass to Ahmad, hopefully catching them off guard. The play works perfectly and we score on a 65-yard pass on the first play of the drive. The McNally fans in the Rose Bowl go crazy!

However, we know USC isn't going to roll over. They have plenty of weapons of their own. By halftime the score is 17-14 with us holding the lead going into the locker room.

When we get to the locker room and gather as coaches, a nasty argument ensues between Click and me. He wants to keep grinding it out, running the ball, to win close. I disagree. "This is USC. Do you really think they can't explode in a minute? We have to use our weapons and go after them hard. If we can't score a bunch of points this half, we will lose," I say. Click responds, "Hell, I've been doing this a long time and you don't get it. The risk is too high to go aggressive on them." At that point, Coach Oliford steps in and says, "Go for it. I am not losing this game sitting on the ball. Make Ahmad the guy this half and let's win the damn game." As usual, he sides with me, which just pisses Click off. This means I am calling plays this half, so I better make something happen.

I pull the offense together before we head back onto the field. "We are going to go for it this half. We are holding nothing back. This is where we show how to finish. Are you with me?" I ask. The players jump up and start shouting, "finish, finish, finish." It appears I got through to them.

We get the ball to start the second half. On the first play, we run a reverse to Ahmad for 30 yards. The next play is a crossing route to Ahmad for 25 yards and you can feel that USC is reeling. Just when they are on their heels, I call a trap play that goes 20 yards for a touchdown. It was a three-play drive for a touchdown and our players are excited. We continue our aggressive approach and score next on a 35-yard pass to Ahmad to go up 31-14. We just keep pouring on the pressure and the points, winning the game 45-21. It is an impressive victory over a very good team.

As I watch Coach Oliford hoist the Rose Bowl trophy over his head, I envision myself in that position one day. I run over to the stands to give Cyndy a kiss and tell her I will call her when I get to Tampa.

As we gather in the locker room to sing the fight song and celebrate, Coach Oliford stuns me when he calls me into the center of the circle. "We talk all the time about learning to finish. I asked

Coach to stay and finish the job here with you guys. Not only did he do that, but he called a heck of a ball game. That's why today, he gets the game ball for finishing and helping us be the best we can be. Congratulations."

I have never been so caught off guard by anything in my life. As I well-up with tears, I hold the ball in the air and say, "I love you guys." With that the singing and the partying begins.

After some brief comments at the press conference, I am on my way to the airport to begin a new life in Florida.

CHAPTER 22

A NEW DAY

One day you are an assistant coach, talking about how you would do things differently if you were the head coach. The next day you are the head coach and now you are that unreasonable prick making everyone work long hours and demanding perfection. It is not an easy transition. You start out with the idea of still trying to be one of the guys. Then you realize they really don't want you to be one of the guys. You are the head coach, so act like it!

Having watched this play out before, I decided from the outset that I wasn't going to try and be "one of the guys." I would assume the role of head coach and understand the consequences. After all, a lot of people are now depending upon me for their livelihood. Ultimately, success is the most important factor.

My first task at Florida A&I is a staff meeting with the assistant coaches. This will be followed by a meeting of everyone involved in our football operation. We must all be on the same page with the same goals and values if we are going to succeed. And by goals and values, I mean mine! There is only one agenda and that is the one I set. No confusion around here. Pleasing everyone is not part of the deal and it will not lead to ultimate success. This will make things uncomfortable at first, but then everyone will adjust. They really have no choice.

The coaches meeting is easy because these are all guys that I have selected and hired. They are solid men and excited to get started coaching. For them, I have two messages. First, close out this recruiting year strong. We cannot afford to start with an average class. Even though we only have a little over a month to get it done, there are no excuses. Second, immediately start getting to know the players here at Florida A&I. We need to make a connection with them as soon as possible. We not only need the players to feel good about us and the upcoming season, but we also need them to help us recruit. These coaches are experienced and will get us started off on the right foot.

The second meeting is much different. This combines all of the rest of the football administration. Trainers, doctors, equipment managers, video guys, clerical staff, and others, are all in the room. I know nothing about any of them and have formed no opinions. That scares them to death. While the coaching staff is secure, I am addressing a room full of people who are totally insecure. I have to walk a fine line here. I don't want them in a panic or nothing will get done. But I also don't want them to believe I am making any kind of commitment to them. I could end up having to fire them all, I just really don't know yet. The best I can do is lay out my mode of operation and let them try to adapt to my set of values. Some will survive, some will not.

"Today is a new day for Florida A&I football. Forget everything that took place in the past and focus on the future. We are going to do great things here, but it won't just happen. We need to attend to the little things. When you take care of the little things, big things happen. I have one simple rule. Do what you say you are going to do and do it now! Nothing irritates me more than a lack of follow through. I won't ask any more of you than I ask of myself, but I won't ask any less either. Nothing in life is guaranteed. I encourage you to go about your jobs with a goal of being the very best. We are going to be one team, speaking with one voice, and focused on winning championships."

With that, I have said what I need to say. It is up to them to decide to get on the bus. If they don't, we will help them pack.

My most trusted guy here is Cal Smith. He has been here since the day after I took the job and has been getting to know the place. This will be the first time we have been sitting face to face to talk about his experience so far. He is a smart guy and very perceptive.

"So, what do you think after almost a month here?" I ask as we sit privately in my new office. "Truthfully, this place is a disaster," Cal starts. "Most of the staff is lazy and entitled. The administration moves slowly. The team has a huge drug problem. Have I cheered you up?" Cal asks. I laugh and say, "Well, they were losing for a reason, and we are here for a reason. The public never knows what it looks like on the inside. Coaches get fired for a reason and you just laid out some pretty compelling reasons."

At that point, Cal and I begin to lay out a plan to replace almost everyone on the staff. My secretary is the bright spot. She has been there three years, long enough to understand the job and know key people, but not long enough to develop bad habits. Cal says his impression is that she is loyal, smart, trustworthy, a keeper. Valerie stays. She may end up being about the only one.

If you look deep into any organization, in this case a football program, you find that there is never just one reason for success or failure. You can look through an entire organization and never completely determine the root causes of the failures. Many of the people here have for years been watching head coaches come and go, never feeling like they were in any way responsible. The new people I will hire will understand that we rise and fall together, and they should not expect to survive if I don't. Everything matters when it comes to putting the entire puzzle together. The sooner we get rid of the dead weight the better.

"Wait until I hit Curt with wiping everyone out. He will go into a panic," I tell Cal. "Coach, I am not so sure about that. He may think the problems around here are the same as you and I think. Don't be defensive when you meet with him," Cal tells me. "I hope you are right. That would make it easier," I add.

About an hour later, Curt Feeny pokes his head in my office to say hello and see how things are going. As we visit, I can see that he has a pretty good grasp on the problems in the organization. When I tell him about the staff, he responds, "Good. We need a clean slate. Just do it quickly so I can sell it to Human Resources as part of the coaching transition. And hire good people. We have a lot at stake here."

When you are the head coach, you become so self-centered, you forget a lot of others have something at stake here as well. Curt just hired a young assistant coach. He has the chance to look like a hero or an idiot, nothing in between. He wants me to be successful. If I do this right, he will be my biggest supporter in getting us where we want to go.

As Curt leaves, I feel good about the situation and the possibilities for this program. Now I have to meet with the players. This might be a tough meeting, especially if we have a drug problem, which seems evident.

There are many ways to handle this. I am direct and I want the players to understand that about me immediately. This first meeting will be meant to excite the players about playing for us and to set a tone for what we will represent as a program. Nothing like a new day for everyone.

At 3 p.m. sharp I walk into the team meeting room. I wanted to see what I was getting into, so I didn't have the coaches prep them in any way. No matter what I was prepared for, it was worse. The players sit in their chairs, many wearing hats, dressed like slobs, and sending a disinterested vibe. It is all I can do to keep from going off.

"Good afternoon men. Today is a new day for Florida A&I football," I say as my voice rises. "Let's start by having you sit up in your chairs and please remove your hats. Hats are to be worn outdoors only, not inside the facility. You want to win championships? You start by carrying yourself like a champion. That means how you look, how you act, how you approach every single day. We will be champions here, but it will take a full commitment from everyone to make it happen."

From there I turn the tables to inspiration about what this can be, their part in it, and the values of our program. I can see in their eyes that I have their attention and they want to be part of this. Well, not all of them, but most of them. Then I hit them with the whammy at the end. "Commitment to becoming a champion means doing everything right. That is why I want everyone on this team to head straight down to the training room to take a drug test." In an instant, you can feel the panic set into the room. Clearly, the rumors were right. We have a drug problem and we need to address it quickly.

They were not expecting this. However, my attitude has always been that the only ones with any angst will be the guys who use drugs. The clean guys, the ones we need to depend on to win, won't have any issue with the test. I am always reminding myself of the advice of a wise man. Don't spend 90% of your time worrying about 10% of your team. Some guys just don't fit and the sooner you both figure that out, the better.

Symptomatic of the issues throughout the program, when the players get to the training room the drug testing is poorly organized. Some players have to wait almost two hours to get tested. I am livid. As the final player leaves, I walk into Cal's office and say, "When I come in tomorrow morning, the trainer better be gone and his office cleaned out. That was an embarrassment."

Today was a new day for many, and unfortunately the last day for some!

CHAPTER 23

WE ARE UNDEFEATED

Like every new coach, the height of my popularity is from the day I took the job through the opening game. It's pretty hard to keep things in perspective when people are telling you how wonderful you are, and you haven't even coached a game yet. Cyndy asked me one night, "Did you ever imagine they would like you so much here?" I respond, "Honey, we are undefeated." We both laugh.

In addition to the coaching and recruiting, much of my time is devoted to being on the road at booster events or doing media appearances. With two little ones at home now, it is nearly impossible for Cyndy to accompany me on very many of these. That means discipline on my part. I am amazed at the suggestive ways women approach me at these events. It's not often even subtle, and many times their husbands are in the same room. I begin to believe that if I wanted to, I would be entertained every night by damn good-looking women. But for now, I have to be extremely careful.

Here is what I do know, it's not fun to cheat if you can't tell anyone. That goes for the husbands who want to do whatever it takes to recruit players, or the wives who want to do whatever it takes to bed the coach. The only guarantee is this, it won't stay quiet. I am smart enough to figure that part out and I haven't even coached a game.

The booster events are important for the purpose of connecting with the people we are going to need in recruiting. Florida A&I doesn't have a group like The Coach's Crew at McNally University. Their system has been loose and sloppy. I like the system at McNally, where the head coach controls the group. Assistant coaches will move on, so they don't need to know everything. Assembling this group is a little tricky, but I am using the first guys I met to pull it all together, Ken Wilson and Ted Morgan. They were in this from the start and have a lot invested in my success. They are the perfect guys.

"What we need is to find 30 guys we can completely trust," I begin. "They will have unlimited access to me, but all of the player dealings go through the two of you. Each one of these guys needs to be comfortable giving at least $50,000 a year with no benefits or questions asked. If they don't have a big stake in the game, they become way too dangerous."

I can see Ken and Ted are excited. They want a strong leader with a plan. This plan is exactly what they have been waiting for at Florida A&I.

"Also, nothing is to be said to Curt Feeny or the President. They should know nothing and any questions they have should be met with a denial. It's best for all of us, and they are both better off not knowing," I add. "This is how we prefer it as well, Coach. The circle will be tight and you will be able to completely trust all of us," Ken says. "Let's start by hosting some dinners, maybe 4-6 people at a time, where they get to know you and understand where we are headed. After those dinners, Ken and I will follow-up and get them on board," adds Ted.

"Perfect. The sooner we get started the better," I say with excitement in my voice. With that, the next phase of the turnaround kicks into high gear.

The next step is establishing good relationships with the media. Usually the beat writers who cover the teams are pretty average and not the opinion makers among the media. I need one of the more influential writers to champion our cause. I have to identify who this is and take him out drinking.

My target is the lead columnist at the local newspaper. He is not a particularly sharp guy, but a graduate of Florida A&I. Everyone thought he would do big things, but he is still here and not going anywhere. His wife has a better job than he does, so they are staying put in Tampa. He has to try and be friendly with the fans because he lives here and plans to stay. That means he will play it "down the middle," writing mostly positive stuff about the program. Like a lot of newspaper guys, he is lazy and pissed that coaches and administrators his age are making ten times what he makes. I will have to neutralize that natural bias. In my short time in Tampa, I have discovered that while his successful wife is working long hours, he is banging a young copy editor at the paper. If all else fails, I've got that tidbit in my hip pocket.

"So, tell me what you think has gone wrong with our program from your perspective," I ask Lee Bradwater in our first session at the Tiger Paw Bar. I am acting like I care about his opinion to stroke his ego. "Well, you have a lot of problems to deal with I think. The program is out of control, there is no discipline, and the players are arrogant. The program seems rudderless," Bradwater explains. Okay, his observations are right on the money and I tell him so.

"You must be pretty perceptive to see all of that from the outside," I respond. "Here is the problem. Most of the public doesn't really know all of that. They know we haven't been winning, but they don't know why. Anything you can do to educate them is appreciated, although I know you have your own opinions to write."

"I would like to see the program succeed. It's more fun to cover a good team than a bad one," he laughs. "I will find a way to tell the story. All I can ask is that you keep me in the loop and give me good access. I don't want to get beat by the competitor," he adds. There you have it. Don't make me work for anything and I will write what you want. Isn't the media a great industry?

"Perfect," I say. "I think we are going to enjoy working together." As he tosses down his third vodka with cranberries in less than an hour, I try and wrap this up. This is the part of the job I hate, having to deal with some loser who I need to write good things. I will have to placate him on a regular basis. For a couple of million dollars a year, I guess I can stand it. As we depart, Lee stumbles out the door and gets in a car driven by a woman too young to be his wife. Poor girl, this will end badly.

One by one, I start to address the various pieces of the puzzle needed to build a great program. It all seems to be going well as I make my way to Channel 8 for the taping of my very first television coaches show. When I arrive, I am greeted by our media relations director, Kevin Johnson, and the host of the show, Mark Ahearn. They take me on a tour of the station, meeting one person after another. The staff seems to think it is a big deal to have the coach in the studio today, which is fine with me.

As we meet various people, we walk onto the news set to meet their popular news anchors. I am seldom stunned by anyone, but the female anchor, Julia Chisholm, is without a doubt the most spectacular woman I have ever seen. She is confident, strong, elegant, and has a smile that knocks me off my feet. I am at a loss for words for the first time in my life. "Welcome to Tampa, Coach. I hope you love it here and have great success," she says, looking directly into my eyes. "We are all fans here and want you to do well."

Like a sophomore who just had the Homecoming Queen smile at him, I respond with some ridiculous nonsense that probably made her wonder how I ever got this job. We exchange a few more pleasantries when she says, "Well, I have to get back on the air. It was a pleasure to meet you." I simply reply, "Likewise."

As we walk away, the sports director, Mark Ahearn says to me, "Have you ever seen such a beautiful woman in your life? Don't waste your time though. Better men than you have tried to tap that without success," he laughs. I reply, "I am a married man, Mark." He just laughs and responds, "I am just saying, she is special, no matter your situation."

I quickly try and move on from that awkward conversation, but I can't get Julia out of my head.

I tape the first show and it all goes well. As I head to the parking lot, I see Julia drive off in her red Mercedes. I can't wait until we tape another television show.

As I head back to the house, all of a sudden, things feel a little different.

CHAPTER 24
HEADING TO KICKOFF

Fall practice is where you start to define what kind of football team you might become this season. We have spent all of spring practice and summer conditioning workouts setting a different tone for the program. By now, we have already dismissed 18 players for positive drug tests. That has significantly changed the attitude of our team. I think a team is like any other group of people, they want treatment that is fair and equitable. When the team lacks discipline, or the rules are not enforced evenly, you end up with very poor team chemistry.

The best time to get the chemistry right is at the very beginning. This means we will have to make examples out of some individuals. Fans won't understand a hard-ass approach in year three, but they understand it and like it in year one. There seems to be a certain satisfaction in thinking that your coach is a tough guy. It gives fans a belief that the team will somehow also be tougher, reflecting the attitude of the head coach.

I have seen different approaches to becoming the head coach. You often hear about the "Players' Coach," which by definition indicates that the players are running him, not the other way around. At first, all the stories of the players' coach are positive, bordering on glowing. Generally, the team performs better than with the last coach, but only for a while. The fans rally around how great this is and how it is all so much better than before. The players are all quoted on how much better things are and how much they like the coach. It is a real love fest. Then the lack of discipline, the lack of accountability, and the lack of respect, begin to become factors. The team starts to perform at a lesser level than anticipated. Then the cracks begin to show and the losses start to mount. What was once the beloved players' coach is now seen as a loser who is too soft on his players. Bad things happen, players get into trouble, and eventually the coach is fired.

This scenario unfolds on a regular basis. I am not going to fall into that trap. I am going to be a complete prick. When the program starts to show the consistent results that I expect, I will ease off a little, maybe!

With our new routine of two-a-day practices, the players really don't know exactly what to expect. I like it this way. I like them to feel constant pressure. The same goes for the coaching staff. I want everyone a little off balance as they get started. We all have high goals and aspirations, but each one of us has to be at our best, which I believe means striving to make every little detail perfect. At practice, I move aggressively from one position group to another, creating angst and intensity wherever I go. The purpose is to keep everybody on their toes all practice long. We have to be able to create a mentality of intensity for 60 minutes.

"That's not good enough. We can't afford to take any plays off, not in practice, not in a game. When I watched film of last year, we took too many plays off. When you do that, you get beat. You practice like you play and right now that is not good enough. I want to find 22 guys who want to do things right on every play. When I find these guys, we will have a damn good football team. Until I do, you are going to have to live with me on your asses every single minute of every single day," I say as I stop practice.

"I am tired of telling you the same things over and over. Listen to your coaches and take coaching. Until you do, we are going to be a very average football team."

Our players are just kids. I don't care what anyone tells you about their size and strength. They are kids who need to be reminded and prompted continually. You know the old expression, "I told you once, I'm not going to tell you again?" Try saying that to a college football team. You will find yourself looking for work before you know it. Constant reminders, constant corrections, over and over.

When we head off the field after the morning practice, the coaching staff gathers in the meeting room to talk about practice. Because he is older and more experienced, Bucky Fox decides he can give his opinion to the group. "It's only the first day, Coach. I think you have to give the kids a little room at the beginning," Bucky says. I respect his opinion and I do get where he is coming from, but I disagree.

"You really think this group needs less pressure? They need more. There is no mental toughness in this group and if you think that a mentally weak team can beat Miami, then you are crazy," I begin. "Does anybody else think we ought to take it easy on the kids?" I ask sarcastically. No coach in his right mind is going to challenge me now. But I give Bucky credit, he doesn't back down. (Which is why I like the way he coaches defense). "That's not what I said or what I meant, and you know that. I'm just trying not to kill their spirit on the first day of practice," he replies.

"We are breaking a bad culture, not breaking their spirit. It's not good enough, you know that and deep down so do they. The worst thing we can do now is let them slip back into bad habits. It will be tense. You have to stay close to your players and keep reminding them where we are headed. It is all about where we are headed, not where they have been. Keep them focused straight ahead, no distractions, one goal. It's your most important job. Got it?" I ask.

As they all begin to leave the staff room, I motion to Bucky to meet me in my office. I need this guy to be really good, and he is. I don't need him pissed off at me. It will affect his coaching.

"Bucky, you know why I did that, don't you?" I ask. "Not really, but you made your point," Bucky responds. "Here is the deal," I continue. "You know what needs to be done and you have been there. You are the best at what you do and I know that. But most of the coaches on this staff are young guys and they have no idea what it takes yet. I was talking to them as much as I was talking to the players. If I had a whole room of seasoned coaches like you, I wouldn't have to address it."

"I understand, but you are coming down pretty hard," Bucky adds. "It wouldn't hurt to tone it down a bit." "I know," I say in response. "But I am going to keep the pressure on. It is up to you and Nick to address the kids who need a little boost. You guys know how to handle that and I trust you completely. Leave the young coaches and the rest of the staff to me. That is where we have to set the culture."

"Got it. I will talk to Nick and we will make sure you get what you want," says Bucky. "That's why I am thrilled that you are here, Bucky. I need you to help us win a Championship," I add.

A leader needs to know how to get the very best from his people. Often times that comes in very different approaches and styles. This goes for the way you deal with players, coaches, and staff. The key to getting the best from your players is knowing which ones need to be yelled at, and which ones need a hug around the neck. If you approach them all the same, you will never win. You might hear a coach say, "I treat everyone the same." Yeah, right! The ones who actually do that don't last too long in this business. The secret is to appear to treat them all the same. The third team guy who misses practice is dismissed for violation of team rules. The star who misses practice is excused to deal with some personal matters. (Of course, you have to wait and talk to him to find out what those personal matters need to be.) Honestly, the players all understand the double standard. Statements like these are for the benefit of the fans.

As we begin to move through fall camp, the change in our team is obvious. Getting rid of the problem players was important, but so was teaching the rest of the players the importance of doing things right. I have made an example of several players by dismissing them from the team (not the best ones of course). Average players are expendable and often pay the price as we instill discipline. We have to get better every day. We cannot stay the same. We either get better or worse. I am trying to instill that culture in everyone, every day.

Curt Feeny stops over at practice a few times a week. He has been terrific in letting me get the right people in this organization to succeed. He and I have what you might term a "get along" relationship. We are not buddies, but we are not foes, we simply coexist. That is probably a good place to be overall.

"What do you think, Curt?" I ask as I jog over to where he is standing. "This is like night and day. The intensity is so much greater, the organization is excellent, and the players actually seem happier. It is exciting to watch," he responds. "Now we just have to get all that to equate to wins. We still have such a long way to go, but they are trying," I add.

I like the fact that Curt will leave practice and tell all the boosters that good things are happening. The boosters are a little pissed because I have barred them from practice, something they are not used to. I have two reasons for doing this. First, they can be a pain in the ass and expect me to spend time with them when I should be coaching. Second, I like making sure they understand who is in control. It may not seem significant, but keeping the upper hand is really a form of intimidation. That is my real motivation. I don't need their input or advice, and the sooner they understand that the better. Curt can now call them with a report from practice, making him look important and keeping them at arms-length from me. You might be surprised what boosters think they should be involved in. Many of them end up damaging programs for years.

Most often, if you look at programs that traditionally under-achieve, you will find a group of boosters who are interfering. People who know nothing about our business should stay out of it, but they don't. I am drawing a hard line which I know means I had better win. When you take a tough position like this and lose, they come after you with a vengeance. Right now, they kind of like telling everyone how hard-nosed the new coach is. That will only continue as long as we win.

Fall camp is the one time of year where you can really enjoy coaching. Of course, I have to do the media stuff daily, which really isn't that bad, but for the most part I am just coaching and meeting with the players and staff. All the other distractions disappear for about a month. It is great.

This also means that I basically disappear from home for a month as well. I sleep in the same dorm where the players stay. It is the best way to get connected to the players away from the practice field. When you are working from 6 a.m. to 11 p.m., there is not much point in going home anyway. It has been hard for Cyndy, raising two young girls with me never at home. I can feel us becoming disconnected, but I am busy so it does not affect me nearly as much.

Taping my weekly television show is becoming the highlight of my week, only because I get to see Julia Chisholm. I find I can't wait for Thursdays, just for a chance to see her for a few minutes. She seems to make herself available then also, which is maybe just wishful thinking on my part.

As we work our way through practice, I begin to have the feeling that we can be a pretty good team. There are no guarantees, but we need to be better than the previous two seasons where they finished 6-6 each year. I can't stand average and that is the definition of average.

My coaching staff is high energy and they are good teachers. They seem to have connected well with the players. They also seem to like each other. Coming from the situation at McNally where there was such tension on the staff, it is a welcome change. We have a lot of work to do and we need everyone pulling in the same direction. When you bring a whole new group of people together, you never know how they will mesh, but things are very good right now.

It helps that I have two strong and experienced coordinators in Nick and Bucky. They set the pace. The other assistants are younger and less experienced, so they are eager to take direction. The players sense the cohesion on our staff and they feed off it.

We have only a few more practice sessions before we play our opening game. But today, we host a pre-season kickoff event starting with a booster luncheon followed by a fan autograph session. This is a fun day for our players and they get out of practice. What could be better?

For me, it's all part of the job and an ego boost. Right now, people are almost crazy with excitement as the season approaches. When the afternoon is over and the last autograph is signed, I send our staff home for the day to be with their families. It has been a hard month for family life.

I head back to my office to shower and dress. I have one last obligation that I have looked forward to for weeks. It is a one-on-one sit-down interview with Julia Chisholm. The focus is a story on the man, rather than the coach. The format is different because it is being done as a news story. Best of all, I discovered the story was Julia's idea.

CHAPTER 25

JULIA

The interview will take place in my office, where the crew from the station is already setting up their equipment. I stop in to say hello to the cameraman and producer, Julia has not arrived yet. In this city, she is like a rock star. For an interview like this, she will be driven over to our practice facility in a Town Car and treated like royalty. All of this makes her even more alluring.

Kevin Johnson, our media relations director, pokes his head in my back office to tell me that they are set to go and Julia has arrived. As I walk into the room, she stands up and reaches out her hand. "Hello Coach, it is nice to see you again. Thank you for doing this, especially on a busy day." She may be a star, but something about her style puts you completely as ease. She exudes both confidence and warmth at the same time. Clearly, this is why she is so popular and has the top-rated newscast in all of Florida.

"Let me give you my thoughts on this interview and what we are trying to accomplish. A new coach comes to town and we all get the football part of this. But you are an important figure in this city and people are interested to find out more about you as a person. How you grew up? How you got into coaching? What your life was like in Ohio? Why here? What was the lure of Florida A&I?

What do you hope to accomplish personally? How do you define success? Things like that," she concludes.

"Well, I don't know how interesting I am, I'm just a football coach," I respond in a feeble attempt to be self-deprecating. "You'll have to help me along to give you what you want, but I'm all in."

"Great. Let's get started and if you need to take a break, let me know," she says confidently.

With the camera rolling, she starts. "How does a young man from a small town in Ohio end up as the head coach at one of the top football powers in the South?"

"I was taught by my parents at a young age to define what I wanted, and then with a single-minded focus, make it happen. I think that is how I got to this point," I start. Now looking directly into her eyes, I say, "When I decide I want something, it has my complete and undivided focus. That is how I achieve my goals." I can tell this answer has made her a bit uncomfortable. She stumbles through the next series of questions, a little off balance. Clearly, she knows that was directed at her, but I would have given the same answer to anyone. It is what I believe and how I approach life. Also, if I ever have a chance with her, I need to get on equal footing. To this point, she has been the star and I am just another fan worshipping her from afar.

The interview gets back on track and for the next hour we talk about everything imaginable. We discuss family, childhood friends, people I admire, and what will be the measure of success. It is such an easy, free flowing conversation, like we have known each other for years. I don't know how it will turn out, but it feels like the interview went well.

Her final question was this. "How will you know when you have reached your ultimate level of achievement here in Tampa?" Fair question. Here was my response. "When we get to the point in all of college football where we become the team to beat. I want us to be so powerful that each team we play will view our game as their

Super Bowl. We want to dominate in every area, every single day." That is putting it right out there, but it is what I believe and I'm not one of those who hides from expectations.

The interview is over and Julia says, "I have never been in a football complex before, it's very interesting." I see an opening and take it. "If you have time, let me take you on a short tour of the place. You really have not seen anything yet," I say. Her eyes light up and she says, "I would enjoy that very much."

Even as we wander through the building, it seems like the conversation is so easy and natural. Before I know it, another hour has gone by and it is getting late. I promised Cyndy I would try and be home at a decent hour. I have hardly seen the girls lately.

As I walk her out to the waiting town car, I say, "this was really enjoyable. It would be great to spend some time together again soon." She responds, "yes, I agree. Here is the best way to reach me." She hands me a card with her cell phone number written on the back.

Good night!

CHAPTER 26

GAME DAY

With all the hype that surrounds the hiring of a new coach, the first game is even more over-hyped. Fans are hoping that a magic formula has been discovered and the team will go on to the National Championship. In reality, first games are not much of an indication of anything. You have a new coach, new offense, new defense, new overall style, and some new players. Overall, it creates the excitement of the unknown.

Today in Tampa is no different. Though the opponent is not strong, Texas Long Branch, the excitement of the opening game and the beautiful blue sky of Florida creates the perfect environment for an opening game. Fans will be in the parking lots early, tailgating and enjoying themselves. They will talk about the team and what to expect. It is one of the things that makes college football so popular, the idea that "this could be our year". Most college teams and their fans generally feel this way, so today is filled with anticipation.

For the coaches and the teams, it is really more a case of staying focused on what lies ahead. Because of all the hype, it is easy to get caught up in things that really don't matter. That is exactly what

I am telling our team as we prepare for the game. The opponent does not matter, what we do matters.

The morning starts with a pre-game meal, which is actually a brunch, since they won't eat again until after the game. Most people would be generally surprised to see how much players eat prior to the game. The pre-game meal consists of food that will provide energy for the day ahead. The players sit with other players at their position and their coach. It is the final time they will be together to review last minute details and reminders. The players appear to be adjusting to our new routine.

I try to remain aware that everything is new for them and this accounts for some of their uneasiness. After a while, they will learn the routine and it will be exactly what they expect. Not today.

"Everyone back down here dressed in coat and tie with your bags packed at 10:50 a.m. sharp," Cal Smith announces loudly to the team. Quickly, they head back to their hotel rooms to rest for a few minutes and gather their belongings. They are quiet, which is an attempt to show focus. We will find out on the field later today.

We gather at 10:50 a.m. in the meeting room, one final time before heading to the stadium. It is my last chance to keep their focus. Pre-game speeches are over-rated. By this time, we are minutes from kickoff so it is really too late to change their focus. But here at the hotel, a couple hours before kickoff, I have a chance. What I say needs to be brief but impactful.

"This has been an exciting year for me. Coming to Florida A&I and getting to coach you guys is special. We have put in a lot of hard work over the past eight months to get ready for this game. However, that will mean nothing if we do not stay focused. There is a lot of hype, I can't deny that. But I need you to ignore the hype and focus on two things, Texas Long Branch and yourself. If each of us executes the little details we have worked on for the past eight months, we will be successful. If not, the results will show in the score. Your coaches have a great plan for this game. Execute their plan. If we do that, there will be plenty to celebrate afterwards. Perfect execution is the goal for today. Ignore everything else."

We play a short music video which has the best examples of perfect execution during our fall practices. The video is exciting, upbeat, and probably the best way to gain the attention of young players. I can see them focus on the video screen for its three-minute duration. When it is finished, we all head to the buses for a short ride to the stadium.

As the Tampa Police escort guides us into the parking lots of the Tampa Stadium, fans are cheering wildly and giving our team the thumbs up. This is pretty heady stuff for an 18-year-old, who was playing high school football just one year ago. This is why I have been preaching focus, over and over.

I still get fired up walking into the locker room and seeing all the lockers set-up with jerseys, pants, shining helmets, and shoes. It means it is "Game Day" and time to see what kind of team we have. As I head to the coaches' locker room, I am also working hard to keep focus. There are a lot of firsts for me today as well. I try not to think about it, but I know the 65,000 fans in attendance today are probably most focused on what they think of me. It is part of the deal and I know it. As much as I try to put the focus on the players, this is the first game for a new coach, and the jury is out. I keep reminding myself that this is a journey and the first game is just another game. But today, it is not. I want to win, and look good doing it, so I need to keep my focus.

When I step on the field for the first time during pre-game warm ups, it feels great. Forget the hype, on the field I am completely comfortable and in the zone. Our team is pretty crisp during warm-ups, a good sign and an indication that our coaches have them well prepared. As we head into the locker room for the final time, I am anxious to get this season going.

"Guys, I have said all that I am going to say. It is up to you to go out and execute for 60 minutes. Let's go." With that, we head out of the locker room for kickoff.

We win the coin toss and in this case, I elect to take the ball. I want to be aggressive and take control early. In some games, you have to account for your gut instinct rather than all the typical kind of coaching rules of thumb.

As we take the field for the kickoff, it is actually the first time I have been able to just relax and do my job. All the hype means nothing once the ball is kicked. It is now about performance and results.

On the first drive, we execute to near perfection, resulting in a 15-yard touchdown pass. The crowd goes crazy because not only did we score, we looked good doing it. The first series on defense is much the same as Texas Long Branch goes three and out and is forced to punt. You can feel the energy in the stadium as they see the difference from one year ago. First impressions are important and so far, we are making a good one.

"We have to keep reminding them to focus," I say into the head-sets to our coaches. "Things are going well, but they will let their guard down if we allow them to. The same goes for all of us."

The next series is a little tougher, but we end up scoring again on a 6-yard run. By halftime, we are up 28-0 and have played well. That means I have to set new goals at halftime to refocus the team.

"I like our focus in the first half, but we cannot let down. We have two goals for this half. A shutout by the defense, and no turn-overs on offense. We need to set the tone from the opening kick-off," I tell them.

The second half goes exactly as we had hoped and we win the game 45-0. It was a good day and the players are excited. After we sing the school song in celebration, I remind them to behave to-night and get ready for next week.

I head into the post-game press conference and my message is simple. I am proud of how we played as a team and it is a good start. But it is only one game and we still have a lot of work to do.

Only one game, try telling the fans that! Right now, I just want to get dressed and head home to see Cyndy and the girls. It has been a tense nine months for our family!

CHAPTER 27

WE NEED BETTER PLAYERS

As well as we played in the opening game, I am acutely aware that we are not yet ready to compete at the highest levels of college football. We need better players and more of them. The fans won't understand this, and I am certainly not going to admit publicly that we need better players. That would destroy morale and end the trust I have built with the current team. It is a common dilemma many new coaches face in their first few years.

For us, the exhilaration among our fans is way too high after just one win. This week we face Florida, who has been one of the top teams in the country for a number of years. The hype surrounding an in-state rivalry game like this one is huge. As a football team, we will be tested in every phase of the game. I can tell our staff feels immense pressure as we need to play the best we are capable of playing, and hope for a little help along the way.

In reality, there is more pressure on Florida than on us. They are expected to win, we are not. But remember, reality and fans have absolutely nothing in common. Our fan base is expecting a win so we need to find a way to win this game.

The coach at Florida is very different than me. He is a fast talking, crowd pleasing, good old boy who makes bold predictions, and loves to take cheap shots at the opponent. His style works for him. He has already won a National Championship and has an excellent team this year.

We are a real recruiting challenge for him however. Our staff is working harder than his in recruiting and we are going head to head with most of the same players. That means he will try and create something around this game to discredit us. We are ready and it doesn't take him long. At his weekly press conference on Tuesday, Coach King told the media, "I like the new young guy they hired at Florida A&I. He seems like he might be able to field a competitive team. That would be good for us because it would make the games more interesting. I think it is good for college football in Florida to have a good second tier type team. It also creates opportunities for the players we can't take to play college football in their own state."

The media goes wild with his statement and they want an immediate response from me. He just called us a second-rate program with second rate players. These things are really ridiculous when you think about it. What can I say that really matters? I am going to stick to my usual style and speak directly to our recruits. They are my most important audience.

"We are excited to play this game. Clearly, being an in-state rivalry adds energy to Saturday's game. We know the very best players in Florida will be watching and we hope they see a program at Florida A&I that they would like to be a part of in the years to come. We are building something special here and exciting days lie ahead," I respond.

What about Coach King calling your program second tier, they want to know? "I think everyone in the country knows that Florida A&I is as big as it gets. We are excited about the future of this program," I add.

I am not going to bite. It's not my style and it will just start something I don't want to be a part of. I know the media and some of our fans would love to have me snap back, but I am not going to play that game. Win in recruiting and win on the field. That is the only way to beat Florida.

I also remind our players to stay away from trash talk this week. It is hard for them because they have high school teammates on the Florida team. Some of our players probably wanted to go to Florida and were not offered scholarships. In-state rivalries create a myriad of emotions for players. I am trying to build a team of emotionless, stealth fighters who go into the game with a mission to win and complete the task. We are making strides in building this mentality, but we aren't there yet. Once we have it, we will be a highly effective team.

This game will be different for our team because we are going on the road to play. With a road game, the preparation routine stays the same, but everything else is different. There are no allies on the road. Everyone is rooting against you from the employees at the hotel where you are staying to the stadium security staff. You generally have to endure lousy accommodations in the locker room as well. It becomes us against the world and I will teach them to embrace this. Right now, it is all new and I am just trying to build enough confidence to not be intimidated. 75,000 fans cheering for the opponent is intimidating enough. You can't be intimidated by the surroundings and let it affect your focus.

As we take the field to warm up, I can see that our players are nervous. Watching the Florida team warm up, we probably have reason to be. They are an amazing looking group of athletes. As we jog back into the locker room for the final time, I realize I need to get this team to relax and keep building confidence.

When I pull the team together, I say this. "Guys, this is not life or death. It is just football. Go out today and execute the way you did last week. If you do, we will have some fun."

We start the game well, taking the opening drive down the field to score. But Florida is just too much for us and they ultimately win the game 21-17. I am actually very proud of our effort and I tell the team that.

However, this game reminds me that we still have a lot of work ahead.

CHAPTER 28

WE NEED PLAYERS

My message to the coaching staff on Sunday morning after the Florida game is simple. We need players.

I thought we had a good game plan and executed pretty well. Florida just has better players than we do. Recruiting is the only way to fix this and we need to focus our efforts on recruiting above all else.

After meeting with the staff, I call Ted Morgan and Ken Wilson to schedule a meeting for later that day. They need to understand that we can't wait to recruit, we need to start now. Both seem happy to hear from me and anxious to help. We will meet at Ted's at 3 p.m. today.

One of the things I have to remember as a head coach is to keep the big picture well in focus. I am realistic enough to know that we will need players of Florida's caliber we are going to beat them. Coaching can be way overrated as compared to recruiting. A lot of average coaches have won with superior players. Very few great coaches have won consistently with average players. Players make the plays, and that is a fact.

When I arrive at Ted's, I can tell immediately they want to talk about the Florida game. Ted starts, "I thought we played pretty well

yesterday. On the road in a tough environment, I am encouraged."
Ken chimes in, "You had a good plan against them. Just a play here
or there would have turned it."

"I agree," I start, "but the reason we didn't win is because they
have better players. Florida has out-recruited us badly and it shows
when we are head to head. Ken, you are correct that a play here or
there could have turned it. But we don't have the players to make
those plays yet." It is clear they both understand and agree with
what I am saying.

"That's why I am here. We need to ramp up recruiting fast and you
and your group are key, " I say. "Florida is on all the same guys and
hitting them hard. Here is the list of the top 20 guys we need to get."

"A lot of schools are doing the same thing you know," Ken adds.
"I get that, so we just have to be better than they are. Our coaches
are working their butts off, but without help from you guys, it will
be hard. Can I count on you to get this moving?" I ask.

"You know it, Coach," Ken says. "Can we host a little get together on Tuesday night over at Ken's so you can tell our group about
the recruits and get them fired up? They need to hear from you.
They are committed, but this is new to all of them."

"Absolutely. Keep it confidential and very low key. I will be happy to lay out the direction of the program for them. This is the
single most important thing we are doing," I note.

The machine is getting cranked up and needs to kick into high
gear.

"Just a reminder. Not a word to the President or Curt. We need
to make sure all the guys know that," I caution. "Done," says Ken.

I like these guys. They seem to get it and really want to help.
It will be impossible to win some of our recruiting battles without
them. I think they like knowing that, too.

On the drive back to the office, I call Cyndy to see how she and
the girls are doing. This has been a tough time with everything
new and me gone all the time. She is being a good sport and it

---

helps that her mom lives so close. She visits Tampa often to be with Cyndy and the girls. I welcome this because it takes the pressure off me.

As I walk back into my office, my private line is ringing, which is odd. No one but Cyndy and my parents call on that line. I don't recognize the number but pick up anyway. "I don't know much about football, but I hope you're not discouraged after yesterday." I immediately recognize Julia's distinctive voice. "Not at all. We just have to get some better players in here and we will be fine. It is nice of you to call," I say. She responds, "I was just thinking about you. I imagine losses are tough. I just want you to know that I am here if you need someone to talk to." Wow, I was not expecting this. Clearly, she's interested in me or she would not be calling. We talk for another thirty minutes and it goes by quickly. When we finish, she says, "Okay, the next call is yours." Part of me wants to call her back right then.

As I head into the meeting room with the players, my head is spinning. I need to snap out of it because we have ten games left and a chance to have a good season. What this team needs right now is confidence and leadership.

"I'm not going to insult you guys by saying how we gave a great effort and came up short. The game is played to win. We are focused on perfect execution. If we do that, we will be hard to beat," I tell them.

My job is to get the very best out of each one of these guys, regardless of talent. They need very direct feedback and a belief that they can do big things. These are great kids and are trying to do everything we ask. In some cases, the skills are just not there.

That is why I am constantly reminding the staff about recruiting. We have to coach this team, but recruit better players. That is exactly what I am going to tell the boosters on Tuesday night.

Late that afternoon, Curt Feeny stops by to check in and say, "hang in there". He understands where we are as a team and that we have to address the deficiencies. What he does not know is how we are going about it. I can't afford for him to find out either. I try to keep him moderately informed on how we are doing, but I can't tell him too much. Part of me wonders if he has some idea what we are up to, but chooses to leave it alone. As the athletic director, he is better off not knowing some things. He is a nice man who is hoping if things get going, he will also reap the benefits. Let's hope we all do!

By Tuesday evening, I am ready for the group at Ken's house. The reality is none of these guys would be my friends outside of this setting. They are alright, just not really my kind of guys. However, they are totally into what I am telling them and hanging on every word. They are thrilled to hear about every recruit. I hope they can deliver.

I issue them a challenge. "Two years from now, when you look on the field, I want you to be able to say, 'I made a real difference'." Their response is excited and engaged.

It's now late, and the 11 p.m. newscast is over. I decide to dial Julia on her cell phone and she picks up immediately. "Still working at this hour? I thought I was the only one," she says. "I was just ready to head home. Want to stop by for a drink?" She is very direct and I like that. "Give me your address and I will be over," I respond.

Then I text Cyndy to say I still have film to watch so I am going to stay at the office. As I head to Julia's, I know things are about to change for good. Once you head down this path, you can never go back. I wonder why I am doing this?

The rest of the season goes well enough to build some momentum. We finish 8-4 and qualify for the Apple Orchard Bowl. This is the best way to start as a new head coach. Our fans see that I can coach, but I don't want to win too much and create unrealistic expectations for the next season. Best of all, recruiting is going very well and we have a chance to sign a tremendous class in February.

I feel like there aren't enough hours in the day. Between the team, recruiting, Cyndy, and Julia, one way or another I am managing to balance everything.

Nothing can take precedent over signing a top recruiting class. This is the key to everything we are building and this final month will either make or break us.

I get regular updates from Ted and Ken. They are very upbeat about their part of the operation. We will see when the stakes get higher.

CHAPTER 29
SIMPLE FACT OF LIFE

This is the simple fact of life in college football. If you have a good quarterback, you win. If you have a bad quarterback, you lose.

The guy we need is at Miami Dade County High School in Florida. He is 6'-3", 200 pounds, runs the 40-yard dash in 4.5 second, can vertical jump 38", and has an exceptional arm. His name is Zeke Bradshaw and is the kind of player that comes along once in a lifetime. Whoever gets him will win and win big!

We have been recruiting him since the day we arrived at Florida A&I, but that still puts us behind schools that have been recruiting him for years. He can choose from any school in the country and he knows it. Our main advantage is that we are in Florida and his family is not wealthy. His dad is an alcoholic who bounces from job to job. His mom works at the school as a Teacher's Aide, making very little money. She is treated well, in large part, because she is Zeke's mom.

Zeke is a nice kid, cocky, but not in an offensive way. He is not your typical 18-year old. Right now, he has the world by the tail and he knows it. Right or wrong, it is pretty hard for a kid to remain grounded when he is this highly recruited. Over the past year, there have been times where I had to hold my breath at many of his comments. That is how recruiting works. To a large extent, grown men have to demean themselves to cater to the whims of high school kids. It's all part of the deal, but the least appealing part of the job. I try to remind myself that I can put up with a year of this because, after that, I own him for the next four.

The first time I met Zeke was last March when he came down to watch our spring practice session. He and I had about an hour together in my office to get to know one another. I felt like we hit is off well. Being 33 years old makes the connection easier. I won't always have that advantage, but for now, I am going to use it.

He is not really a selfish kid, but he wants to make sure he goes somewhere that will benefit him, not just where he will benefit the program. I get that. This is a kid who could one day sign a $100 million NFL contract, so his goals are a little different from your average high school senior. If he can help us win a National Championship before he heads to the NFL, I'm all for his personal goals. I told him as much in our very first meeting.

I think being honest with kids is the best way to build a relationship. They know a phony and will dismiss that guy quickly. Too many coaches end up acting like a used car salesman which I believe turns kids off.

Today is a completely different experience because I am going into Zeke's house for my one allowable home visit. You never know exactly what to expect on these visits. Also, until you have gone into the home, you don't have a complete understanding of the player. Most people would be amazed at what some of these kids deal with on a daily basis. In this case, the mom does not worry me, but the dad is a wild card. Nick Sallee and I show up at the front door, prepared for just about anything.

They live in a small row house in a rough section of Miami. I have certainly seen worse, but this is not great by any stretch. Zeke answers the door and is very polite as usual. He takes us into the living room of the house where his parents are waiting for us. His mom is quiet, but very warm as we are introduced. His dad is loud and aggressive. It doesn't take long to figure out he has spent most of the afternoon drinking. I can tell Zeke is embarrassed, though he is probably used to it by now.

"You should be so proud of Zeke. He has put himself in a position to go anywhere he wants to get a great education and play college football," I begin. "We would just like to make sure that happens closer to home, like Tampa." We all laugh at the obvious point of our visit.

"I could really care less about the school part of this. Zeke has big talent and he needs to get ready for the NFL. He won't need a degree to make a ton of money there," his dad blurts out. His mom, clearly embarrassed, says, "I want to make sure he gets an education. Neither of us had one and I don't want to let that happen to Zeke." (The last thing we need is tension in the family.)

"I can tell you this, we will do both with Zeke. He won't have to choose. We can have him take summer school each year while he works out. When his junior season is over, the first time he can declare for the draft, he will already have his degree. NFL teams will really like that," I finish. Everyone seems both relieved and impressed with the idea.

The conversation continues to go well but I want to get Zeke away from the dad for a while. "How about you and I go for a walk, Zeke? Coach Sallee can stay here and spend some time with your parents."

"Sounds good. I can show you around the neighborhood," Zeke says, seeming anxious to get out of the house as well. I know Nick. He'll have a few drinks with the dad to seem like a regular guy, eat some of Mom's homemade cookies, and make them both comfortable with us. If Ted's crew does their part with the parents, we will be in the game. There are just a lot of "ifs" right now. I need to convince Zeke that I will help make all his dreams come true.

"What do you think of all of this recruiting by now, Zeke?" I say as we walk along the street. "It's okay. I just feel bad when I'm not interested in a school and have to tell them no. Some are cool, some get nasty," he tells.

"Well I hope we aren't one of those schools, Zeke," I say with a laugh. "Oh, no Coach. I really like you and Florida A&I. It is fairly close to home, but just far enough away. I think you will do big things there and the players I know all think you are great," he responds.

"That's good to hear. Now let's talk about you," I say. For the next hour, we walk and talk and he is very open with me. This is exactly what I hoped would happen from this visit. I want Zeke to be so comfortable with me that it will be hard to tell me no. I understand recruiting at the core. A lot of head coaches have been away from it for so long, they forget the importance of connecting with the kids.

As we head back in the house, I hear Zeke's dad laughing and Nick telling a story. Mission accomplished. As we all say goodnight, I leave with the feeling that we have a good chance to sign Zeke, the best player in the country.

As we climb in the car, Nick look at me and says, "thanks for leaving me with that asshole." We both laugh as I remind him, "it's all part of the job, Coach!"

When I get back to the hotel that night, I call Ted. "We had a great visit. From what I saw of the dad tonight, your part of this will be important. Just have the guys make sure they get him in the mornings. By the afternoon, he will probably be hammered," I tell him. "I would also leave the mom out of this. I think she is a really nice person and probably would rather not be a party to anything. She will be more interested in getting back and forth to his games. She and Zeke are pretty close it seems, so location plays to our advantage in this instance. The dad is just looking at dollar signs."

Before I head to bed, I call Cyndy on my university cell phone to check in and say goodnight. Then I take out my private personal cell phone to call Julia. Florida has open record laws that allow the media to access your phone records when they choose. I can't have her number start appearing on a university phone record request, thus the private cell phone. We talk long into the night before we both finally fade.

The next morning, we are on a private jet flying to see two more great players, a running back in Georgia and a defensive lineman in Louisiana. I have the entire month scheduled like this. Thank heavens for the Learjet. It makes travel so simple and effective. Every player I am seeing is a difference maker and a key part of the big puzzle we are putting together. It is very exciting, but it is a high stakes game. Everyone cheats, it's just a matter of who is better at it.

The upcoming weekend is highlighted on my calendar because it is the weekend that Zeke Bradshaw makes his official visit to our campus. To a large extent, what happens on this visit is "make or break" for us. We can overcome an average visit, but not a bad visit. Because we are rebuilding, Zeke needs to see that the program is on the right track. Most importantly, I want him to feel good about our players.

We will host Zeke and his parents on campus for only 48 hours, so it must be planned perfectly from the time he steps foot on campus, until the time he leaves. Cal Smith is the master at planning these weekends. He picks the right player to host Zeke, and makes sure the recruits are "properly entertained". He has a knack, and he has a network, especially among the female recruiting hostesses that we hire to help us. Some of these women are so committed to Florida A&I football that they will literally do anything to help. We need everything we can muster this weekend to make a great impression on the Bradshaw family.

I flew back late last night so I could be in the office today, making sure all the final details are in place for Zeke. This guy is the key to our future success. When you sign a great quarterback, the other recruits seem to fall into place quickly. I have seen this happen many times.

As expected, Cal has everything down to a science. Zeke's host will be Julian Brown, a wide receiver from Miami who we signed last year. Julian is excited about our staff and more importantly, he needs a great quarterback to throw him the ball. He is the perfect host for Zeke.

When the family arrives at the football complex, we have everyone waiting to greet them. It may be a little over the top, but we want to make an impression. We will tone it down as the weekend goes along, but right now the family seems to like the attention.

"We will take you over to the hotel to check in and then head to dinner. Nick, put all their stuff in my Escalade. I will drive them to the hotel," I instruct. "Follow me," I say to the Bradshaws. "We will look around for a minute before we head to the hotel." I give them a brief tour of the facility, just to give them a taste of what we have to offer.

As we drive to the hotel, I give them a quick tour of the campus. "After I drop you off, I am heading home to get my wife Cyndy. I am anxious for you to meet her and she is excited to meet you all. The place we are going for dinner is Tony Roma's. You like ribs?" I ask, already knowing the answer. "Yes sir," Zeke says. "They are my favorite. I haven't been to Tony Roma's, but I have heard they are the best."

"I would say second best. Cyndy makes the best. A girl from Birmingham knows how to cook ribs. Come to Florida A&I and she'll make them as often as you want," I joke. We all laugh and everyone seems very comfortable.

When I get to the house, Cyndy and the girls are waiting for me. It is great to see them in the daylight. Cyndy's mom is there helping out, which relieves me. Cyndy looks fabulous and her smile is infectious. The Bradshaws will love her. The girls are growing up so fast. It seems like they change so much from week to week. As a coach, you almost forget how little you are home. Your kids don't forget though, and they are starved for your attention when you are home.

After an hour, we kiss the girls goodnight and head to pick up the parents. Julian Brown will pick up Zeke and meet us at the restaurant. Cyndy is in a very talkative mood and she seems excited to be with me and to help recruit. It's like she thrives on this, which is great for recruiting.

As expected, the Bradshaws are completely taken with Cyndy. She has a way of making everyone feel great. Zeke takes to her immediately and she promises to make him ribs every week.

The players head off on their own and, after several drinks at the bar, we take the parents back to the hotel. Cyndy is excited to be out and having drinks with adults.

Once we have dropped the Bradshaws back at the hotel, Cyndy snuggles up next to me in the car. "Think the girls on campus will make Zeke feel welcome tonight?" she giggles. "I'm sure he will have a lot of fun tonight," I respond. Cyndy reaches over, unzips my pants, and says, "He shouldn't be the only one who has fun tonight," as she buries her head in my lap. I'm not sure what brought this on, but it's a great way to end the night.

When I see Zeke at breakfast, he seems happy as can be. I ask Cal how it went last night. He jokes, "I think a lot of great girls got to know Zeke last night. He was a big hit."

The rest of the day is spent in meetings and campus tours. That evening, Cyndy and I host everyone at our house for dinner. I like to have everyone to the house because it is a warm setting and both parents and recruits seem to enjoy being there.

By Sunday morning, it is time to start pressing the recruits and closing the deal. They have had fun, seen the campus and the facilities, gotten to know our players, so there should be no reason to keep them from making a commitment. We have good success in the early meetings, securing six commitments from really excellent players. My last meeting is with Zeke.

Before I can even start, Zeke says, "Coach, I love it here. Everything feels right. But I have two more visits and I feel obligated to fulfill those commitments." Smart kid. He comes right out of the box hitting first. It is hard to argue with his sentiment or obvious character.

"Zeke, I get that. Just promise me you won't do anything until you and I have a chance to talk first," I ask. "You got that, Coach. Another school would have to do something really special to beat this place," he adds. That is exactly what I am worried about!

As they head to the airport, I realize that we have got to get this closed quickly. I call Ted and say, "we can't afford for this to go on much longer. We need to hit him hard this week. This guy changes everything."

On Tuesday night, I get a phone call from Zeke. "Coach, I've decided I want to be at Florida A&I. I am cancelling my other visits and announcing it tomorrow." "Zeke, that is so great. We are going to be champions together. This is a great day in Tampa," I say.

Nick calls me within ten minutes. "Did Zeke call you yet?" "I just got off the phone with him a few minutes ago. Great work, Nick," I add.

"I really don't know what the hell happened. Out of the clear blue, he tells me he's coming for FAI. I about fell out of my chair. Whatever happened, it is a great thing," Nick says excitedly.

I hang up the phone, and dial Ted. "I like a man who can close a deal. Congratulations," I say!

CHAPTER 30
IT ALL STARTS TO CLICK

I can feel a difference in our team as we take the field for spring practice. No longer is everything new and the routine is more comfortable for the players and coaches. The coaches now know what I want from them, and the players know what the assistant coaches expect from them. Everything moves faster and I can feel the energy and the pace rise a notch. It is what I had hoped would happen in our second year.

Off the field, the pressure on me personally is starting to build. Dividing time between Cyndy and Julia is tricky. Julia is starting to expect a little more out of our relationship. It is clear that while she doesn't expect me to leave my wife, she does expect to be treated like a queen. She has decided that she wants a spectacular apartment on the water. Even though she makes a lot of money on her own, she makes it clear that I should expect to pay at least part of this upgrade. I need to figure out how to do that without any paper trail.

The group of guys Ted and Ken put together is getting it done for us in recruiting, but they are also becoming a little more demanding of my time and attention. They are decent guys, just not the type I want to hang out with regularly. Still, I need them to help us get players, so I have to give them what they want. Tonight, I have a big dinner with this group at the Country Club where I will review where we are headed as a program and what to expect next fall.

Sometimes I look back and think, how did I get headed down this path? But then, reality sets in. I want to win more than anything else in the world. That is the justification. I have been able to keep a clean public reputation, but in my profession, other coaches know exactly why we are getting players. It's hard for them to say anything though, because they are likely cheating as well. Turning your head in this business is in the best interest of everyone.

The other looming issue is the type of kids we are taking. It's not a big secret that 90% of the best college football players would never be able to get into college on their own merit. They are usually the product of a special admissions committee. With a lot of academic support and tutoring, they can stay eligible, though it is not easy. Many often end up being the worst students in every class!

Then there are guys who, in addition to not being great students, live on the edge constantly. They are most often your best players, but a case could be made that they just don't belong in college. We all know that they will never get a college degree. In fact, many have zero interest in a college degree. They are the ones you worry about every single day and night. Is this the day they do something crazy? But they are also the game changers on the field. I worry about them constantly, but they are a big part of what we need right now.

Year two means the fans are ready for some significant wins. It takes a while to build a program, but most fans don't want to hear that. They want things to start happening now.

Additionally, my relationship with Curt Feeny is a bit strained. He and I have a good public working relationship, but generally no personal relationship. He is a smart guy and I think has figured out something is going on with Ted and his group. No matter how confidential you try and keep things, it seldom works. He's not ready to confront me on this because he is not sure, and he knows I will just deny it. Plus, if he looks into it too closely, he will be implicated because he was the one who hired me. I tend to get reminders like, "I'm sure you are doing things the right way. We are going to give you time to build the program so you don't need to cut any corners," he will say. I know he means well and really does not want us to cheat. But at the same time, he knows how competitive it is out there and he wants to win.

I'm sure my personal life has been talked about among the leaders at the University. These would only be rumors, but of concern to the President and athletic director. The past few times we have been at social functions, Fern Twillie, the President's wife, has been unusually cold to me.

The President probably figures there is not a lot he can do, especially since rumors about him and his PR gal run rampant. That may be part of the reason his wife is so edgy about this. I'm guessing that some people are in Guy and Curt's ear about this. However, it is hard for them to address, especially if they have any idea who the other person is. Julia has a huge following in Tampa.

On the other hand, Cyndy remains the constant and even keel part of my life. She and girls are actually no stress. They are happy and content in every respect. Cyndy built her dream home, an 8,000 square feet mansion on the water. She and her mom have spent a small fortune decorating it. It is a great place and perfect for team events and recruiting dinners. I still can't believe I own a home like this, but it is terrific.

Cyndy continues to be a star at all the public events and in our recruiting process. Our relationship is not the same. I spend a lot of nights at the office. But we have fallen into a good groove, adjusting to this new job. That part of my life, and being on the field, are the two most normal parts of the day. I spend much of my day worrying about the next potential issue among our players. When you are dealing with 120 college kids, disaster seems to always be just around the corner!

The biggest difference going from an assistant coach to a head coach is the demands on your time from the public and the media. You seldom deal with either group much when you are an assistant coach. The coaching part seems the same and is for me the greatest release. Once I am on the field, I can forget about everything other than football.

We have recruited a spectacular running back who is able to enroll mid-year. He will be here for spring football practice. He is a big, strong kid who grew up on the streets of Philadelphia. He is an angry, tough guy, which is part of what makes him special on the football field. I am concerned that he will always be on the edge of trouble. But, players like Alonzo Fuller are hard to find. I remind our coaches to keep an eye on him all the time and try to minimize the issues. He is not particularly close to anyone, so we never really know who he might be hanging out with. This scares the hell out of me. When I first started in this business, I swore I would never have guys like Alonzo on my team. Then reality sets in, and you know what you need to win games. I need Alonzo Fuller.

I have to constantly sell the President and others on the fact that Alonzo is a good kid who just needs an opportunity. The group that really doesn't like him is the faculty. They are smart and complain constantly to the Provost about the kind of kids we are bringing in. But let's be honest, the public doesn't care who we bring in. If we win, everyone is fine with whomever we have on the team.

Alumni will say they want to be proud of the kind of program we run, and the type of people on the team. In reality, winning trumps all. That's a fact!

As I watch our team progress during spring practice, I can feel the difference. Things are starting to click.

CHAPTER 31

ONE STEP CLOSER

As the second season approaches, I can feel the momentum start to build. We have a good team, and young players who will be the foundation for future success. Public expectations are high, but not unreasonable. I have tried my best to tone things down, but I can only control so much.

Our players have begun to gain the kind of focus that it takes to be special. The other thing I like is that our players have begun to take more ownership in the team. I have always believed that the players must become totally vested in the outcome of the season to be successful.

We are starting a freshman quarterback which will create some growing pains. However, Zeke Bradshaw may be the most mature freshman I have ever been around. Even as a first-year player, he has command of the locker room and command of the huddle. The transition for freshmen to play major college football cannot be taken for granted. The level of competition is dramatically better. You have to be a special guy to deal with all of it, especially as a quarterback. A year ago, he was in high school. Now he is leading his team onto the field in front of 65,000 people and a national television audience. Pretty heavy stuff for a young kid. I have complete confidence in Zeke, but we will see what happens when he actually takes his first snap!

The adulation that comes to a player like Zeke is almost hard to comprehend. Before he ever stepped foot on campus, he was one of the most recognizable players in the South. Everyone wants to meet him, touch him, or shake his hand. At our "Fan Day", the line to get his autograph stretched the length of the field. True to form, he stayed until every last person had the desired autograph. Grown women act like silly coeds around him. Grown men act like they are meeting a rock star. It's really hard to watch.

For whatever reason, Zeke stays very grounded through all of this. That gives me hope he can remain calm and focused when he is under center in a game. If he is the player we believe he is, we will have three pretty special years before he leaves for the NFL. You don't get this chance very often and we are going to make the most of it.

This season we start with a big game right out of the gate, opening at home against Tennessee. It is not the ideal way to break in a young team and a freshman quarterback, but our focus throughout fall camp has been excellent because of the magnitude of the game. Tennessee is, historically, a great program and we can gain real credibility by beating them. Being at home is big for us, not just because of the fans, but because of the familiarity of everything. This will provide a springboard for a great season if we can find a way to win.

One of the advantages of new players and a young program is that we are less predictable than an established team. Tennessee has been winning by constantly doing the same things on offense and defense for the twelve years that Mike Silvestry has been the head coach. His program is defined by continuity and consistency as most of his staff has been with him his entire career as a head coach. They are not fancy, but they have good players and execute to perfection. This will be a real challenge for us.

In some ways, our young guys are not at all intimidated by a team like Tennessee. They have no base of history with them, so they approach this game like they would any other team. That may be naïve, but it may prove to be an advantage. I can tell you Zeke Bradshaw is intimidated by no one. It's not an arrogant attitude, just one of complete confidence. Clearly, our team feeds off his swagger.

The hype around this game is something I have tried to downplay for a couple of reasons. First, I want to take the pressure off our team. The reality is we are the underdogs and a win would generally be unexpected. If we lose this game, I don't want it to break our spirit and cause more losses as the season progresses. Second, I want to let Tennessee come in here without any chip on their shoulder. As the saying goes, never poke a sleeping bear.

However, as hard as I try to limit the hype, an opening game in prime time on ESPN against Tennessee is a big deal. There is no hiding that fact.

I have been in big games, but this one is a little different. ESPN wants to put a mic on me in the locker room for my pre-game talk. When Coach Silvestry and I meet in the middle of the field pre-game to say hello, there will be cameras everywhere. It is really quite annoying. Yet I know this is part of the deal, plus, potential recruits may be watching this game to get a feel for me and for our program. It is the kind of recruiting opportunity that is priceless, so I need to be at the top of my game.

I forget about the ESPN microphone as I call the team together before taking the field. The players will sense if I am sincere, or putting on a show for the camera. "Guys, this is what we have been practicing for since January. Finally, we have our chance to go out on the field together and show the world what we've got. I like the way you have prepared. Your focus has been good. But maintaining that focus for 60 minutes will be the key. This game will come down to the last few minutes, and the team with the most consistent focus will win. Decide right now to play one play at a time, executing to perfection, and take the fight to Tennessee for 60 minutes. The only thing that matters right now is what we think. The men in this room will determine the outcome of this game. I'm excited to see you play. Now let's go win a football game." With that, the room explodes, and we head for the tunnel to the field.

As we take the field the place is absolutely crazy. It's the opening game of a new season, we are playing a big-time opponent, it is a beautiful day, and we have a new quarterback. All these things add energy to an already electric atmosphere. When we get to the edge of the field, I turn around and look into the eyes of our players. The young players' eyes are mostly glazed over. They probably can't believe they are here. The older guys seem focused and ready. When I look into the eyes of Zeke Bradshaw, I see complete calm. His steel-eyed look of a warrior gives me great confidence.

Unusual for me, when we win the toss and I again elect to take the ball. I want to get Zeke out there as soon as possible so he gets a feel for the game.

On the first play from scrimmage, we hand the ball to Alonzo Fuller, and he carries for six yards. The second play, I let Zeke throw the ball. It is a safe play for 8 yards and we get a first down. You can feel that we are gaining confidence with each play. As we drive down the field to the Tennessee 30, I tell Nick, "Let's see what our boy can do. Throw the skinny post and let's try and score here."

Zeke drops back, calm and cool, and tosses a perfect strike right into the hands of Julian Brown, and we score first. The place is electric as our fans start to think what it is going to be like to have such a special player on our team!

When Zeke gets to the sidelines, I ask, "how did it feel out there?" In his typical way, Zeke says, "They are fast. We are going to be in a dogfight all game. I have to stay focused." Perfect! He is not overly excited and realizes this will be tough. Add to that the fact that Tennessee is moving the ball down the field on our defense and is about to score and answer back.

Now reality sets in. We are going to have to control the clock and keep putting points on the board if we are going to win. By halftime, Tennessee leads 24-21 as we head to the locker room. When we get inside the coaches' locker room, I snap. "We haven't stopped them yet. Either we have a bad game plan or you are doing a lousy job of getting them into position," I shout at Bucky Fox and the defensive staff. I'm pissed and they know it. "Get it fixed. I better see a different defense this next half." I have been good to these guys, but that performance was ridiculous. They are accountable and better start getting it done.

The second half is one heck of a game. Both defenses are better and the yardage comes harder. Alonzo Fuller continues to pound ahead and now has over 100 yards rushing. As we head into the fourth quarter, we are tied 38-38. This is the point at which Zeke Bradshaw grows up right before my eyes. He takes the offense down the field like an NFL veteran on his way to a winning drive. With 52 seconds left, he again hits Julian Brown, this time on a 25-yard pass to the corner of the end zone to secure the win. The place erupts as we head off the field into the locker room. Waiting for me are President Twillie and Curt Feeny, both ecstatic with the win.

When we get to the locker room, I tell the team, "Men, I'm proud of you. You went out there and stood toe to toe with one hell of a team, and you did it for 60 minutes. That is going to be the hallmark of this team. We play to the end and we finish strong. Now, let's sing!" As the team sings the school song, celebratory congratulations fill the locker room.

When I get to the coaches' locker room, I check my text messages. There are hundreds from all sorts of people, but only one I really care about. It is from Julia. "No matter how late, I have a little celebration planned."

CHAPTER 32

LIVING A LIE

I wake up every morning never exactly sure who I am. I am being celebrated as the coach, a winner who is the perfect family man, just the kind of guy you want your son to play for. It's like the old adage, "Men want to be him, and women want to be with him." The reality is, I'm really neither one. I have perfected only one thing and that is constantly lying.

It is hard, though. People begin to make me believe that I am really special and that I can do things that no one else can do. But deep down, I know the reality. I'm making several million dollars a year. I'd probably be lucky to make $50,000 a year in another profession. So much of what goes on in sports is a mirage. Coaches have a short shelf-life, so I make the most of everything whenever I can, both personally and professionally. All of the sudden, I wake up one morning, look in the mirror, and find I don't recognize the person I have become.

I start to rationalize everything. It's not my fault, I am just playing the part they want me to play. It's not me, it's them. They are the real culprits. But deep down I know that I have become everything I despised as a young man.

But, I'm not going to give up the money, the Escalade, the big house, the woman on the side, the free dinners, the free trips, and most importantly, the near hero worship from the public. I have everything and yet I really have nothing.

Don't get me wrong, I realize I could put an end to all of this. What really bothers me is that I have no desire to do so. The lie has become a part of the fabric of my character and it is not easy to correct that behavior.

With Julia, at first it was mostly infatuation on my part. She seemed perfect in every way. Smart, beautiful, talented, interesting, exciting, and the sex was spectacular. It was like I just could not get enough of her. Now, all those things are still important, but she has also become the person I trust most in the world. That used to be Cyndy, but she is busy now with the kids, the house, spending my money, (which pisses me off, but who am I to say anything) and busy playing the role of the head coach's wife. She is beloved in Tampa and has her own cult following. Our time together is more routine and necessary than enjoyable. Her mom is always here and she has a ton of friends. I suspect she thinks I may be messing around a little, but doesn't seem overly concerned about my comings and goings.

My secretary is really in a terrible spot. I'm sure she has figured out everything, but is too loyal to say anything to anyone. I pay her well and give her little bonuses, which she knows are meant to buy her silence, even though I have never said that explicitly. She is good to me, even helps me keep things straight so I don't walk into a mess. She shuts down the inevitable rumors that I am not exactly "Mr. Clean". The wrong person in her job can fan the flames, the right person can bring it all to a halt. Valerie is the right person, and I am very fortunate. Both Cyndy and Julia like her and trust her, which is helpful to me. In truth, she probably thinks I am a total scumbag!

As I said, no one should feel sorry for me. Everything is a result of my own doing. I want it all, and right now I am pretty much able to get that.

When you start to cut corners however, you start to cut corners in everything. I am living my life on the edge, both personally and professionally. But, it seems like that's how coaches win big in college football. Losing is for losers, so I will do whatever it takes to win. I don't like losing, and I don't like losers. That is my message to everyone I come into contact with. I can tell the assistants get the message. Some are willing to do whatever it takes to stay here and reap the rewards. The others will leave and end up some place where the pressure is less and the stakes are lower.

I think some of my attitude has been magnified by the influence of Julia. She is just as cut throat as I am. She is a top news anchor, with no husband or children, and she likes our arrangement. She likes being in a position of power and being with me gives her the feeling that she is in the game with another fierce competitor. She doesn't get emotional about anything. I know what she wants and I like giving it to her, no strings attached (except for this damned expensive apartment). She makes plenty of money, but she wants me to feel like I have to earn it and paying for part of the apartment is one way of doing that. It is a complicated, yet uncomplicated relationship that is constantly on my mind. I don't really worry about people finding out. We would both just deny it to everyone. It wouldn't be good for either career. No matter what, it pushes me further into a zone that makes things seem almost unreal.

I worry the most about the NCAA knocking on our door one day. Different from the situation with Julia, the guys who are helping in recruiting don't know how to keep their mouths shut and love to tell everyone they are involved in "fixing the program". I know there are rumors in the coaching circles about what we are doing, but these rumors only get credibility if someone on the inside starts talking. It's not fun to help cheat unless you can tell your buddies, and claim a little credit for success. When you are winning, everyone wants to claim a little piece of success. Ted is careful to remind his group of the pitfalls of loose lips, but it is hard to control a group like this. They are all successful, wealthy guys.

I also have begun to worry a little bit about the players. Once you start paying guys, it does two things. First of all, you are at the mercy of those players to some extent. Secondly, the guys who are getting nothing are irritable. They know they are also a big part of our success. You have to spend a lot of time on team chemistry to make it all work. It's something a lot of coaches forget. These are just kids, but kids are more sophisticated today and they don't take everything at face value. You also have to walk a bit of a tightrope to keep the stars from becoming the decision makers. I have a reputation as a hard ass, but the reality is Zeke Bradshaw and Alonzo Fuller can, to a large extent, either make me or break me. I know that and they know that. It is not easy for me to stay in complete control of my team.

Zeke is a great kid and not a big concern of mine. Alonzo is really a bad guy and could go off at any minute. I worry about his relationships with women, which appears very volatile. I remind his coach, Oscar Savage, to talk to him about it every day and try and keep him under some degree of control. He is one heck of a player and we need him to win. We just have to keep his anger under control if possible.

Everything in my life is teetering on the brink of greatness or disaster. One event could send it either way. When you are living a lie, nothing is real, it is only imagined. I am completely living a lie!

CHAPTER 33

DISASTER STRIKES

Things are really on a roll for us. We have won three straight games and we travel to Minnesota this weekend to play an important game on the road. We continue to be a very potent offense because we have a great young quarterback and a powerful running back. Alonzo Fuller is almost unstoppable. I have said before he is an angry guy. That is part of what makes him such a fierce football player.

The game against Minnesota goes perfectly as we win 45-17. Alonzo has 185 yards rushing and has become a powerful force. As we land back in Tampa, I remind the players once again to use good judgment and stay out of trouble. We have too much at stake so I hope they are listening.

I head home feeling pretty good about the progress we are making as a program and our football team in general. As I fall asleep, I feel the most relaxed I have in some time.

When the phone rings at 4 a.m., it can never be a good thing. I hear the voice of our running backs coach, Oscar Savage, on the line. "Coach, Alonzo is in jail. They say he went home last night and beat up his girlfriend. I'm headed to the jail now." Just when we have things going in the right direction, something like this happens. It will be a national story because we are playing well and

Alonzo is having a great season. I need to find out what happened and then decide how to deal with it.

I wake Cyndy to tell her what has happened. She immediately says, "I don't care what the situation was, if Alonzo hit a woman, you have to get rid of him." She is right and I'm sure that will be the sentiment among nearly everyone. Hitting a female is just unacceptable. As I get dressed to head to the office, a million thoughts are running through my mind.

I wait until 8 a.m. to call Curt Feeny about the situation. It's the kind of call you hate to make as a coach. "Get the facts, but act swiftly," Curt advises. "This isn't the kind of thing that can linger on." I try to slow things down a little. "I just want to make sure we give the kid a fair shake. We don't know a lot," I say. Curt says, "But if he hit a woman, that changes everything."

Once I am in the office, it is pretty clear what happened. Alonzo discovered that his "on again, off again" girlfriend has been dating another guy. He went to a bar where she was with this guy and became enraged. In a matter of minutes, things got very violent. At this point, the police arrived and took Alonzo to jail. As Oscar Savage and I discuss this, it becomes clear that Oscar is siding with Alonzo. I said, "we need to get him out of jail and back here. Let's call Ted and see if he can get someone, not directly connected as a booster, to post bail for him." "I am on it," says Oscar.

By this time, the media has the story. Kevin Johnson, our media relations chief, appears in my office asking what we are going to say in response. "Let's hold off for a little while. I haven't even talked to the kid yet," I tell him.

Cal Smith bursts into my office and is pretty worked up. "Coach, we have to act quickly," he says. "We have too many good things going on to let this kid screw it up. Besides, we all know he is not a good guy. You can't hesitate on this one."

"I just want to give the kid a fair shake. I haven't even heard his side of the story yet," I respond. "There is no other side of the story. He hit a woman and the reasons do not matter," Cal exclaims. This bothers me because two people who have tremendous judgment, Cyndy and Cal, have both said to get rid of him. Yet, I know we need him to win games.

Oscar reappears. "I have his release in the works but we may not be able to get him out until tomorrow."

Now I have a decision to make. Do I go ahead and make the call without talking to the kid? It almost seems like I have to. I get Kevin Johnson, Oscar, and Cal in my office. We include Curt on a conference call as well. "I am going to dismiss Alonzo from the program. Let's get it announced as soon as possible. I wish I could talk to the kid, but I will just have to let Oscar relay the information to Alonzo." Everyone leaves my office except Cal. He looks directly at me and says, "I know this is hard, Coach, but you are doing the right thing." I know he's right, but this is still a lousy deal for everyone. I pick up the phone and call Cyndy, who of course, applauds the decision.

The national media seems ecstatic over the decision and the swift action. However, this becomes an omen for the coming days.

For 24 hours, it seems like everything is running smoothly. By noon on Monday, Oscar Savage has Alonzo in my office and the kid is begging for another chance. I'm sure Oscar has coached him up, but he says all the right things. When he leaves, Oscar says to me, "Coach, doing the right thing doesn't win championships. Alonzo can help us win a championship. Don't forget why he is here. We might be just an above average football team without him." He is right, I know that, but I have already made the decision. I can't really change that now. Oscar also reminds me, "Alonzo knows a lot and we don't need him out there talking." Oscar is right again. This could all blow up in my face.

At 5 p.m. I call Kevin Johnson into my office without telling anyone else. "I am changing my mind. We are just suspending Alonzo and we will have him go through anger management counseling. When the professionals tell me he is ready, he will be able to rejoin the team." Kevin warns me that the media will kill me over this decision. "I am aware of that," I tell him.

Within an hour, Cal is in my office. "What in the hell happened?' He asks. "I changed my mind," I respond. "This is a terrible decision, Coach. I can't believe it," he says. "Well, you don't make the decisions around here, I do," I add. Cal storms out of my office.

Within minutes, Curt Feeny is in the office. "I can't believe you did this without telling me," Curt says. "The President is pissed and wants to see us in his office right now."

By now we have a media firestorm and I have gone from hero to goat. As we head to President Twillie's office, I need to think of some way to explain this to him. Curt and I already have a fairly strained relationship. This has made it irreparable.

"Coach, you know we have tried to support you in every way we can, but this is really hard for everyone to take," the President begins. "I want you to reconsider."

"President Twillie, I understand and respect your position on this matter. But he is just a kid, and one from a bad situation. I just want to give him a second chance. If he doesn't complete the counseling appropriately, he won't come back," I explain.

We talk for almost an hour and neither side will budge. It's a little tense as we leave the office. When I am alone, I call Ted Morgan on my cell phone. "I need your help. You guys need to put pressure on Curt and Twillie to leave me alone. We all have a lot at stake here," I tell him. Ted gets it because he is right in the middle of everything.

The next several days are brutal. The national media shows up at my Tuesday press conference for the sole purpose of portraying me as "a win at all cost" coach. It seems to me that no one, inside or outside the football building, agrees with me on the decision. The lone exception remains Oscar Savage.

The one person who understands it, even if she doesn't agree with me, is Julia. "You've got to do what you've got to do," she says.

"Winning is your goal and he can help you win." Honestly, that is it in a nutshell.

Now I have to find what will seem to be a legitimate counseling center, but one that will make sure we get Alonzo back on the field in reasonable time. We need to win games and he is a key to winning.

I have now lost my base of support on campus, so winning is the only thing that matters. Everyone knows you can't touch a winning coach in college football.

CHAPTER 34

THE SEASON CONTINUES

With Alonzo Fuller suspended, we are a good team, but, as Oscar Savage predicted, not what we once were. The entire season has turned a little odd. Most of the media coverage seems to center on the controversy surrounding Alonzo and the incident.

Certainly, my relationship with both the media and the administration has become strained. Ted Morgan, Ken Wilson and their crew have pressured the President into backing off, something the media is killing him over. Curt has basically lost all his juice because it is clear he isn't making the decisions in athletics. For me, it all boils down to winning games. If I do that, most people will forget about this incident and celebrate the success. This may be the only business where you can literally win your way out of problems.

As we play Florida in the seventh game of the season, I know we are in for a real challenge, especially with a weakened running game. Our guys fight like crazy, but we lose the game 28-14. Losing to an in-state rival is never great, but with so much happening, it generates more vocal passion than ever before. Those who want Alonzo to play think we blew an opportunity, which is quite likely true.

I wake up the following morning to the realization that we have to get Alonzo back on the field as soon as possible. We have another tough game this week against Auburn, and it will be a struggle without him.

In many ways, I feel like I have damaged myself with the team. They don't really like Alonzo and he is the polar opposite of everything I have been preaching to them. It is hard for players to know for sure, but if they sense they are playing for a phony, they have a real hard time being loyal. I think some of the guys are beginning to question whether I am a sincere guy or not. They also don't like the appearance of playing favorites, which clearly is the case.

The game against Auburn is much like the game with Florida. We end up losing 20-17. We have gone from unbeaten to 8-2 very quickly, and have dropped from 7th to 18th in the national polls. I have to do something.

On Sunday morning, I pull Cal, Oscar, our trainer, Pete Lively, and Nick Sallee into my office. I tell them that we are "going to war" to get Alonzo back on the field.

"I want this counseling center to clear him on all the anger management stuff today or tomorrow, and I want him on the field by Tuesday. Got it," I tell them.

Pete Lively, the trainer, is in total panic. He will have to be the one to pressure the counseling center into clearing him. "I'm not sure how far I can push them if they say Alonzo needs more time. During the last conversation I had with them, they indicated he was a long way away from being healed," he tells me.

"I'm not asking you, I am telling you. Get it done. If you can't, I will find someone who will," I say angrily. He gets up, leaves the room, and heads downstairs. Everyone else, not really knowing what to say, gets up and leaves also. Before they do, I remind them, "Not one word to anyone about this. I don't need some administrator screwing this up."

The more the day goes along, the more pissed I get. Those two losses easily cost me $500,000 in bonuses, maybe more. Don't these people get it? We are trying to win games, not run a summer camp.

At about 9 p.m., Pete Lively, the trainer, reappears in my office. "At 10 a.m. tomorrow, the main counselor will sign off on Alonzo's release from the program. None of them think he is ready, but they are all fans and understand why he is so important." I can tell he is relieved, but probably not happy to be in the middle of all this.

"Good job. I always had confidence that you could get it done," I tell him. As he leaves the office, he turns to me and says, "I just hope he doesn't hurt anyone else in the meantime." He just couldn't resist telling me I am a jerk. I can't help but admire him for that!

I call Cal into the office and tell him what is happening. I know Cal is opposed to all of this, but what is he going to do? He has a family to feed and is now tied to a guy who can take him to another level in college athletics. His options aren't good, but they are very clear.

"You know the President and Curt are going to be furious that this is happening," Cal tells me. "That's why we aren't saying anything. Your job is to keep Curt away from me for the next 24 hours until the worst of this dies down. Can you do that?" I ask.

"I'll do my best," says Cal, "But Curt is already pissed and this will send him over the edge." He's right and I know it. But remember, this is all about winning and if we win games, he will be powerless to deal with me. Over time, this will prove to be the right strategy for me.

By 1 p.m. on Monday, the word has leaked out and things are wild. Everyone is trying to get the story and a reaction. I go sit in the film room with the quarterbacks, knowing Curt won't interrupt me in there. I know however, that Cal is getting an ear full from him right now. I just don't want to deal with that right this minute.

When we finish practice, there must be 50 reporters, television cameras, and radio people waiting for me. I see that Curt Feeny is waiting for me. He rarely stops by the practice field. Kevin Johnson, our media guy, wants to give me some suggestions on what to say. I ignore him and walk right into the gaggle of media and simply say, "Alonzo has been released by the counselors. I think he deserves a second chance, so he will be out here at practice tomorrow. I don't have anything else to say." I turn and walk away. I ignore the blitz of questions being shouted my way and head straight for Curt.

"Let's go to my office to talk. I don't want to talk in front of these idiots," I tell him. By now, Curt is livid. I have put him in a terrible position and completely disrespected him. I decided I can't worry about that. We need to win games and we need Alonzo to do it.

"I don't even know what to say," Curt begins. "You are telling everyone, including myself and the President, to go to hell. You don't run this University. These are institutional decisions."

"If I win enough games, Curt, yes, I do run this University and you know it. Save me the lecture. You hired me to win games, and that's what I am going to do. If you cross me, I will let everyone know that you are trying to keep us from succeeding. Boosters and fans won't accept that. You really don't have a choice, Curt. You know you have to play the company line and go along with me on this," I finish.

There is total disbelief in his eyes as he turns to walk away. "You are without a doubt, the biggest asshole I have ever met," he says as he turns for the door.

Cal comes into my office and says, "Coach, I hope you know what you are doing. You have really burned a lot of bridges around here."

"You let me worry about that. Just make sure Alonzo is ready to go tomorrow," I remind him.

A few minutes later, I am surprised to see Cyndy standing in the door of my office. "Have you lost your mind?" She starts. "You didn't even ask me what I thought before you did this. Have you become so arrogant you don't listen to anyone else anymore?"

"I didn't want you to worry about it. This is my decision and I'm the one who has to account for it. There are a lot of factors here, including money, which does affect you and the girls. Alonzo will help us win, and winning is the secret to keeping this job. You know that," I tell her.

"I never want you to do the wrong thing just to keep this job. We will be fine. What has happened to you? I feel like I just don't know you anymore," she adds.

"You don't understand the pressure to win. I have to do what I have to do in this instance," I say.

The growing divide between the two of us has been evident for some time. In the early years, I would have consulted her on this. Now, honestly, I never even thought to call and get her opinion. For a moment, that makes me sad, but then I come back to the realization that we are doing this to win.

When I am finally alone, I pick up the phone and call Julia. "Do you mind if I come over a little later? I have to get out of here for a while," I say. "I'm off the air at 11:30 a.m. I will see you after that. You are doing what you have to do. Don't feel bad about that. Sometimes you have to put everything else aside and just focus on the goal," Julia reminds me.

I think to myself, she is cold hearted and driven. Has she rubbed off on me, or have I rubbed off on her? Either way, she is the steel-eyed warrior who gets me refocused every time. Tonight, it will be important to keep my focus. Every day from here on out gets harder.

CHAPTER 35

WINNING

Alonzo is back practicing with the team and the difference is evident immediately. There is a weird vibe in the program right now. The players know we need Alonzo, but they don't feel very good about what all has happened. Additionally, their team is now viewed in a negative light nationally, not because of anything they did.

His first game back, Alonzo rushes for 191 yards. The crowd goes wild and we win the game 45-14. It is obvious what a difference he makes in our team.

The next game is against Florida State, another in-state rival, who is currently undefeated. This will be a good test for us, and a win would propel us into a New Year's Day bowl game.

During this time, my relationship with President Twillie has deteriorated badly and the relationship with Curt Feeny is non-existent. They are both in a difficult spot however, because the fans are so excited about our resurgence since Alonzo is back on the field. They are dreaming about the possibility of bigger things ahead.

I have thought about making an appointment to go see the President, but at this point, I have charted a course that relies on survival by winning. There is really no conversation that will make things better. He is hearing from people on both sides, but the more we win, the harder it is for him to control me. I know he knows that. If he wants to keep his job, the big salary, the mansion, the driver, and all the benefits, he needs to play to the Board of Trustees and the donors. He's really no different from me when it all adds up.

My relationship with Cyndy continues to deteriorate as well. We play the role in public settings and she manages it perfectly. At home, when I am there, we are living two separate lives. Maybe after the season we can get back on track, but right now she seems to simply tolerate me. The girls are fabulous and she is doing a terrific job of raising them. However, I am gone so much and see them awake so seldom, that my relationship with them is minimal. They are probably closer to Cyndy's dad than they are to me. That's not to say they don't love me, I'm just not much of a factor in their lives.

As we prepare for Florida State, I feel a growing confidence in our team. If we can win this game and a big bowl game, we will have a chance to be a National Championship contender next season. I haven't said that to anyone, but Nick and Bucky have seen good teams and they know we have a chance to be special. For Nick and Bucky, winning will put them in a position to land their own head coaching jobs. There is a lot at stake for everyone.

We have an advantage playing Florida State at home. The place is packed and completely out of control. In-state rivalries are unique because families have divided loyalties, and co-workers and friends have bragging rights on the line. It could also impact what some of the top recruits will decide. This game is the epitome of hype.

In addition to all of this, ESPN is doing Game Day live from Tampa, taking the energy to a whole new level. While the Game Day stuff is great for recruiting, it also means that all of the issues surrounding Alonzo will be re-hashed on a national stage. In other words, with the good comes the bad.

As we prepare to take the field, I look into the eyes of our players and see a look of complete focus. They only see winning as an option. What they have gone through this season has changed them in a manner that plays out well on the field. In some ways, I have taught them that winning means everything and losing cannot be tolerated. They take the field with a focus I have never seen before.

From the opening kickoff, our intensity and focus shows. We take the ball down the field 80 yards to score. Zeke Bradshaw is picking the FSU secondary apart throwing the ball. Alonzo has five carries for 45 yards and scores the first touchdown of the game. The stadium in wild!

The defense is just as impressive with a three and out on the opening series against an FSU offense that is currently leading the nation. I told Bucky before the game to let it rip and he is doing just that with blitzes and his scheme. We really have nothing to lose and Florida State is trying to win the National Championship. By the end of the first quarter, it is pretty clear we are an even match for them. In the second quarter, we are able to control the line of scrimmage and we lead 20-17 at the half.

When I get to the locker room, the place is wild. The players are yelling and screaming. They can't wait to get back out on the field and play the second half. They have the focus and confidence of a team that wins championships. It shows in the second half as we go on to win 41-31, a very impressive victory on national television.

After the game, I head down the stadium tunnel and see President Twillie and Curt Feeny waiting for me, all smiles and congratulations. What a couple of frauds. They are playing right along with winning.

In the locker room, I tell the team, "this is all about winning. You do whatever it takes to win the game. Never let anyone else tell you anything different. Now, we have a chance to play in the Orange Bowl and make a statement. Start getting ready today because we are going to dominate that game, got it?" With that a cheer goes up and the fight song starts. We are on a mission and there is no stopping us now. We are still a young football team, but with a bowl win, we will be favored to win the National Championship next season. We have to do whatever it takes.

After the game, Cyndy and I head to a big party at Ted's house to celebrate the season. There is back slapping all around and the liquor is flowing. Amazingly, there is not one mention of Alonzo and the situation. It probably helped that he had 152 yards and three touchdowns. Obviously, the cure for all sins still remains winning!

As I predicted, we dominate the Orange Bowl game and beat UCLA 45-21, setting us up as the national title favorites for the following season.

On the plane flying back to Tampa, I remind each assistant coach that we have to finish recruiting strong, whatever it takes. We are so close to being an elite team.

As we exit the plane, I kiss Cyndy and girls goodbye, telling them I am headed to the office. I climb in the car and head straight to Julia's for the rest of the day.

CHAPTER 36

PRESSURE

Once the bowl game was over and we had closed out an excellent recruiting year, it was time to start making more demands. As I walk into Curt Feeny's office, I have a notebook full of things I want done before the next season. It is an extensive list.

I could tell right away he was taken back by the magnitude of the requests. It is everything from significant facility improvements, to coaching salaries, to recruiting and travel budgets. All total, it is about a $25 million request.

"Do you have a priority order for getting these things done?" Curt asks. "Yes, I want them all done before the season starts," I respond.

"We are talking about a lot of money, especially when we just spent almost $100 million on facilities in the past few years. We will try and do as much as we can, but we are going to have to raise a lot of money," Curt tells me.

"That's not my problem, it's your problem. I'm just trying to win a National Championship and I need these things," I explain.

"Let me get to work and see what we can do," Curt says willingly.

I'm sure he plans to start getting things moving, but I can't take that chance. As soon as I leave his office, I call Ted Morgan on his cell phone. "Ted, I am trying to get some improvements pushed through for the program and Curt Feeny is blocking them. Can you guys put some pressure on him?" "Sure, we need to help you in any way we can," Ted remarks.

Of course, this is not fair to Curt. He is not blocking anything, but I want to make sure it gets done, and to remind Curt that I can create problems for him if it does not. It's a nasty way of doing business, but this is a high stakes game and the pressure is on me to deliver.

Some of the requests are pretty "over the top", but I decide to push hard and see what I can get done. Once you have some leverage, you need to use it.

Everywhere I go, the fans are excited and expectations are through the roof. I have been in pressure situations before, but nothing compares to this. I find my temper is short and my relationships with nearly everyone have become very poor. I keep telling myself that I haven't changed, it's just that the expectations are high so I need to keep the pressure on others. The atmosphere around the office is so intense, it probably drives all of the assistants crazy. But you know what, I'm trying to win a National Championship.

I can feel a big change in my relationship with the coaching staff, even Cal. Everything is much more businesslike on almost all matters. We are on a mission and it has become a cold, focused quest.

While I still do all the fan and booster related events that I am required to do, I find myself hating them. Getting dressed and heading off to speak to some group or attend a fundraiser has become complete drudgery. I find myself looking for the first opportunity to sneak out the door. The only place I really like being right now is at Julia's. She is the only one who is not needy and pressuring me in some way.

I miss everything our girls are involved in. I'm sure other parents wonder if the girls even have a father. Cyndy reminds me of that all the time, which I resent. I don't know what it is but I just can't seem to get my life in order. Yet knowing all this, I do nothing to correct the behavior. It's like I am living someone else's life in my skin.

As we begin fall practice, it is evident that we have a chance to be a very special team. All the pieces are now in place, and the path in front of us is clear. Just win games.

I find myself becoming a bigger and bigger tyrant on the field. I am short and dismissive with everyone, except the players. I still understand that I need the players to make this work and I can't let them start to feel the pressure. If they do, it will affect their play. I think I have done a pretty good job in this area, even if it is insincere. Keeping the pressure off the team is one key to winning.

We open the season with a huge game against Texas A&M at home. It is the ESPN Game Day featured game. I sense our team is excited for the game, but I am very nervous. If we lay an egg here, it will be hard to recover. Opening games are often strange. Both teams have new players and a lot of time to prepare in the off season. A&M has a new quarterback so we don't know exactly what to expect. The fans are so jacked up it's like the whole season is on the line today. The staff feels the pressure. They have spent a hundred hours preparing for this game. At our pre-game meal, I can feel everyone start to tense up, even the players. This is a big game, but we can't start out nervous or tense.

Before we take the field for warm-ups, I do something I have never done before. I call the entire team together in the locker room.

"Men, you are going out there in front of 65,000 people who are living and dying over this game. We aren't living and dying over this game. It's just one step on our road to doing something special. You have prepared well, you are the better team, your coaches have a great plan, that's how we are going to win this game, not on hype. The only thing that matters is what the men in this room think. No one else. I think we are going to have a lot of fun today and we are going to kick their asses!"

You can almost feel the pressure dissipate as energy fills the room. Today is going to be a great day.

Cal comes over to me and says, "Coach, that was awesome. Now enjoy yourself today, too. You haven't been doing that much lately."

He is right. I don't seem to be enjoying much of anything these days, which is strange, given all the good things that are happening for our program.

We start fast with Zeke Bradshaw on fire. He throws three touchdown passes in the first quarter, positioning himself as a Heisman Trophy favorite. We lead 21-0 in what was supposed to be a very close game.

When it is over, we win 45-7 in shocking fashion. The locker room is a happy place, but these guys expected to win so it is more like business as usual, in many respects.

When I get dressed and leave the locker room, I head out to meet Cyndy and girls, but today they are not there. Nick Sallee's wife, Beth, says, "Cyndy told me to tell you she had to leave, but will see you at home. Everything is okay, don't worry." I am worried. Things have not been great between us, but she has kept playing the role and has been good about this.

I dial her cell phone. "Are you okay? Are the girls okay?" I ask. "We are fine. This is just really your thing now, not our thing. The girls were hungry and just wanted to come home. Will we see you tonight?" she asks.

"Yes. I have to drop by a party at Ted's and then I will be home." She hit me right between the eyes. It's no longer "our thing", which means she is totally detaching.

I hang up just long enough to look down to see my dad calling. Suddenly, I realize I haven't talked to him in a few weeks. I have been so busy getting ready for the game.

"Hey Dad," I answer sheepishly. "Congratulations, son. That was a terrific game. You are off to a great start," he says. "I'm sorry I haven't been calling you and Mom. I got so focused on this game," I say somewhat defensively. "Oh, don't worry about that. You know Mom and I understand. You are very busy. How are Cyndy and the girls?" he asks.

"They are fine, but I haven't seen a lot of them lately. It's been pretty crazy around here," I explain.

"Well, don't forget to take good care of them. When everything is said, and done, family is really the only thing you can depend on. The rest of this is not real, just moments in time," Dad says calmly. "I will. Tell Mom hi and I will call soon," I finish.

My dad is a smart man, but I have always assumed he doesn't really get it. He is a high school coach and can't possibly understand the pressure I am under. Other times, I realize that he sees things I can't see because I am too close to it. I have done a poor job of keeping him close to me during all of this.

As I head off to the party with the donors, I keep thinking about what my dad said. Maybe none of this is actually real. I just don't know anymore.

I get to the party and everyone is euphoric, already counting the days to the National Championship game. Typical fans! For some reason, I am just not in the mood for the ramblings of rich guys who have had too much to drink and shrimp breath. I do what I have to do and then sneak out the back door.

I send Julia a text message. "I need to head home tonight. I'll call you in the morning." Her response, "I hope everything is okay. See you soon." She is smart. No need to pry too much. Obviously, I have a reason for heading home, though I am still not sure what is pulling me there.

Cyndy seems surprised when I walk in the door. "Party bad?" she asks. "No, I just wasn't in the mood for it. I thought I would come home and see you and the girls," I say. "The girls will be thrilled that you are home. They are in the living room with my mom and dad."

I almost forgot that her folks are here. Great! I think her mom knows I am a jerk, and even her dad probably wonders why I am such a bad husband and father.

The girls are excited to see me and that relieves any of the tension that might exist.

"Do you guys mind babysitting so I can take Cyndy over to the Country Club for dinner?" I ask them. "Not at all. You two go have some fun," her dad says.

Cyndy looks shocked. "I guess I will go get ready then," she says. I like the Country Club because they will put us at a table away from the crowd and people there, generally, leave us alone. We don't talk a lot until we sit down at the table.

"I am sorry. I know I have been a complete jerk for some time now," I begin. "This job is consuming me and I am not acting like myself, I know that. You hit me hard today when you said this was now my thing. It has always been our thing together. This is my fault and if you will let me, I want a reset."

"I can't really argue with anything you just said, to be honest. But I would like to get back to the way it was also," she responds.

For the next three hours, we talk about everything. It is very refreshing for me and she doesn't ask about Julia. Maybe, she doesn't really know. We have a great evening; the best I have had in a long time.

The next morning, I wake up feeling like a different guy. The pressure is still there, but in a different way.

CHAPTER 37
A MAGIC SEASON

There are times when everything just comes together, and this season seems to be one of those times. The season also provides more opportunity for me to "hide out" in the film room or at practice. I have some public and media obligations, but I can always excuse myself to watch film. No one wants to keep the Coach from coaching.

Our staff is doing an excellent job and we are dominant in all of our games. Sure, we have had a few close calls, which is to be expected. But we won each of those games.

Zeke Bradshaw is tearing it up and it would take a miracle for him not to win the Heisman Trophy.

I am still doing the balancing act overall, but my relationship with Cyndy is close to being back to normal. My relationship with Julia is still good, though I find her "eye of the tiger" view of the world less appealing as it once was. I also find myself needing her less and less.

After we close the regular season, winning the Conference Championship game in fairly convincing fashion, we are selected as the No. 1 seed in the College Playoff System.

In the meantime, I spend much of my time traveling with Zeke Bradshaw to the Heisman Trophy Dinner, the ESPN Awards show, and many other events. In every poll, I am selected as the National Coach of the Year. I give my usual speech. "It's all about having great players, great coaches, and great fans. They are the ones deserving of this honor." This line sells well and makes a lot of people happy.

Our opponent in the semi-final game is Ohio State. They are also undefeated and playing extremely well. For this game, I want our players to be very well prepared, but I don't want them to feel pressure. They need to do what they have been doing all season long.

For that reason, I spend most of my time leading up the game with the players. I have complete confidence in the coaches to have the team prepared. But to be at our best, the players need to be both excited and relaxed going into this game. I love being around the players. It reminds me of when I first got into coaching when I spent 90% of my time with the players. I miss that part of coaching. Head coaches get pulled in so many different directions that sometimes the players are lost in the shuffle. I am determined that is not going to happen during the playoff stretch. The players seem to notice and are responding positively.

I see my cell phone ringing and it is my agent, Jimmy Stallworth. I pick up and he says, "Man, are you going to make a bundle. Florida A&I wants to sign you to a long-term extension and five other schools have already called offering to pay you whatever you want. If you want to stay there, I can make you the highest paid coach in college football."

It takes a minute to sink in. I guess I assumed I would get an extension, but it never occurred to me what the potential numbers might be.

"Jimmy, you go ahead and start working on the deal. I want to concentrate on this next game and hopefully another one. I don't want my contract to be a public discussion while we are still playing. I will tell people that I have not talked to anyone here about an extension, and have no interest in any conversations while we are in season. Got it?" I say.

"You got it. I will get this put together for when the timing is right. Now go win a couple of games. That will drive the price higher," Jimmy laughs.

My Dad has probably never made more than $50,000 a year in his life. Now I am about to move into the multi-millions. In so many ways, it is overwhelming.

As we finish practice, I see the usual swarm of media gathered to ask the same questions they asked yesterday. It's not their fault, it's their job. They are probably as tired of me as I am of them. We slog through the usual stuff until Lee Bradwater, the columnist, asks me, "when you were a young boy growing up, did you ever dream of one day being in the spotlight like this?" Fair question, but not one for which I have a really good answer. "Honestly," I start out. "I dreamed of one day being like my daddy. He is a great dad, great husband, all the players respect him, and he is a nice man. I guess that is what I dreamed about."

"Do you think you have achieved that?" Bradwater asks. "I guess others will have to answer that question," I respond. As I leave the field, I can't get that question and my response out of my head. I wonder if my dad and mom are really proud of what I have become?

By the time we finally arrive at the Semi-Final game, it seems like we have been at this forever. The weeks have drug on to the point where you just want to kick the ball and play the game.

As we get ready to take the field, I remind the team, "There is no next game unless we play this one to perfection. We have not really been tested this season. I guarantee you this, we will be tested today. You fight hard for 60 minutes and ignore the scoreboard. Just make the next play. Let's go have some fun."

Ohio State is similar to us as a team and they are loaded with talent. Their players are strong, fast, confident, and they have not really been tested either. Much of what happens today will be the result of which team is mentally tougher.

The first half goes back and forth, every play matters. When we come in at halftime, the score is 14-14 and the statistics are almost identical. I tell our offensive coaches, "We need to run the ball this half. That's why I took so much shit to keep Alonzo on the field. Control the ball and keep it on the ground. That's how we are going to win this thing."

In the second half, even with a Heisman Trophy quarterback, Nick does what I asked and focuses heavily on rushing the football. It is easy to get impatient, especially in big games, but we are going to stay the course.

Alonzo plays like a beast, pounding it up the middle against a great defense. I know this, given enough chances, he will break one. There is nothing more demoralizing to a defense than when the opponent can run the ball against you.

Midway through the third quarter, it happens. Second down and six, Alonzo breaks through the line, going 44 yards for a touchdown and our sideline goes crazy.

At the end of the third quarter, Ohio State answers back on a trick play for a 33-yard touchdown. Great call by the Buckeyes.

As we head into the fourth quarter tied 21-21, I tell Nick, "You pound the football until they can't take it anymore. Then let Zeke win it for us." "You got it Coach," Nick responds.

Still tied with three minutes to go, our offense has been consistently running the ball. Alonzo has almost 200 yard on the ground. Then I hear Nick call the play, second down and five on our own 40-yard line. They play is a deep post pattern. Zeke hits the receiver in perfect stride for an electrifying touchdown. Perfect call, perfect execution.

The defense holds Ohio State all four downs. We take a knee to end the game 28-21.

We are going to the National Championship game with a chance to make this magical season the best in school history.

When I walk out of the locker room, I see Cyndy and the girls waiting for me. I'm not sure they know exactly what all this means, but I do.

CHAPTER 38

THE BIGGEST GAME OF MY LIFE

Nothing could have prepared me for the spotlight that surrounds the National Championship game. For one week, it seems like it is the only event happening in sports that fans care about.

I am trying to keep some appearance of a normal routine, but that is just not possible. I start with major press conferences every day followed by practice sessions in front of 100 members of the media. Everyone at the school and in the city of Tampa wants to be a part of this particular game.

The players all hear about the various movie stars and celebrities who are coming to the game. It's a surreal experience for all of us.

Our opponent is Stanford. They are also undefeated and a tremendous football team. The media will dissect every part of each program from top to bottom, pointing out every strength and weakness. They will compare coaches, and how each of us will handle both the pressure of the game and the notoriety of the big stage.

The game will be played in Dallas at a state of the art stadium with a video board that stretches the length of the field. It will be an atmosphere like none of us have ever experienced. I tell the team, embrace the moment.

In some ways, I think it has been such a wild road to get here that the players are just enjoying the opportunity. In general, kids handle these things better than the adults.

For me, I have a few people I want at this game. My family, of course, particularly my mom and dad. Also, my college football coach.

When I call Coach Starr to invite him and his wife to be my guests, he is very touched. We have a fairly long conversation and I tell him, "thank you for the way you coached me and treated me in college." He responded, "You have the kind of blind ambition that I never had. That is why you are in this game. You will do whatever it takes to find a way to win. We are all so proud of you." I know he meant it as a compliment, but it's clearly how he and others see me. In the coaching world, to earn respect, you must win above all else.

I know my parents are excited. Their son is the most talked about coach in the country and on television every night. That is pretty neat for parents to see.

When they arrive in Dallas on Saturday before the Monday night game, I ask my dad to take a walk with me. As we head off through the neighborhoods near the hotel, it feels so good just to be with Dad again. I haven't really done this in a long time. I always used work as an excuse.

I tell Dad about the question the columnist asked me about my dreams growing up. He said with tears in his eyes, "I read what you said about me and it made me feel like all I had done to this point in my life was worthwhile. It was the best compliment you could have given me." "Well, I meant it. But when he asked me if I thought I had achieved that dream, I said that was for others to judge. How do you think I have done, Dad?" I ask.

"Son, you have been on a much different path than I was. I am just a high school coach. You had bigger aspirations and ambitions.

That's okay, don't feel bad about any of that. But I would say this, if there are things you think need to change, they are completely within your control. It is never too late to become the person you really want to be," he says simply.

And just like that, as only my dad could do, he puts it all in perspective. It's never too late to become the person you really want to be.

As we near the game, I find myself becoming more and more detached in a lot of ways. It's almost like none of this is real. My head is spinning with hundreds of thoughts and it's almost like I am thinking about everything but the game. Don't get me wrong, we are preparing our butts off. But my private thoughts are all over the map.

The Stanford Coach, Charles Hint, is a terrific guy. He is a younger guy, like myself, and seems to do things the right way. He has been at Stanford for eight years and now has them in the National Championship game. It is a great success story.

As we both wait for the final press conference to begin, we are alone in a private room. I ask Coach Hint, "Are you having any fun?" He responds, "Honestly, not one bit. I had more fun when I was a graduate assistant at UCLA." We both laugh. "I was just thinking the same thing," I reply.

Here we are, both about to coach the biggest game of our lives and neither of us is really enjoying it. The public would be shocked to know that. In some ways, this has all gotten so far away from the reasons we first got into coaching.

After the press conference, I look down to see that I have a text message from Julia. She has decided that she wants to come to the game. This seems odd to me because she doesn't even come to our home games. I guess everyone wants to be at the biggest game of the year. She is bringing her brother, who lives in Atlanta, with her. Maybe it was his idea. Overall, I am not real excited about this because it adds further complications to a lot of logistical issues.

I pull Cal Smith aside because he knows everything anyway. "Julia is coming to the game. She needs to sit as far away from Cyndy as possible. Can you make that happen?' I ask.

"You got it, Coach. Don't worry about this in the least, it is handled," Cal assures me. I've put him in an uncomfortable spot many times. I wonder what he really thinks of me?

Game day is finally here. We can now do what we came here to do in the first place, play a football game.

Here I am, waiting to play the biggest game of my life and trying to figure out why I am not more excited. I have already sacrificed a lot to get here so it seems like it should be more satisfying. I can't think about this right now. We need to win a football game.

As I walk off the field after our warm-ups, I think about my speech to the team.

"Guys, forget about everything else. This is about family. We are playing today for all of our families sitting in the stands, for our football family who has worked so hard together to get us to this point, but most importantly, for the family of men in this locker room. We are going to win this game. When we do, we are going to celebrate. I can tell you this, years from now we will gather to celebrate again. There are 100,000 people sitting out there today in the stadium and millions watching on TV. But the only people you will want to see years from now when we gather, will be each other. That's what family is, the one group you want to be with above all else. We are going to win or lose today based on execution and consistency. But whatever happens during this game, this family cannot be broken. You all deserve to win a championship together. I love each and every one of you." With that, we head out to the field for the biggest game of our lives.

As I walk with Cal, I ask again about the seating. "It is all taken care of Coach. Cyndy and the girls are on the 50-yard line behind the bench with the coaches' families. Julia is on the 50 on the opposite side," he says. "Thanks Cal, I won't forget it."

I laughingly say, "Good thing the asshole President took the luxury suite. I'd be in one hell of a spot." We both laugh as we head to the tunnel.

The game itself is not what anyone could have anticipated. We are on fire from the first play, building a 28-7 lead at halftime. Everyone is stunned, but we are playing great football and at this point, it would be hard for Stanford to come back.

The second half is much the same, minus a couple of Stanford touchdowns when we have our second team on the field. The final score is 49-21, a stunning final for a National Championship game.

As they get ready to make the trophy presentation, I see Cyndy and the girls being ushered onto the field to be with me. What a great sight. It suddenly dawns on me the situation I am in. I turn to the opposite sideline and see Julia. She gives me the thumbs up, then waves, a gesture that seems to be a final goodbye.

As I hug and kiss Cyndy and the girls, I now know exactly what I want to do and where I want to be.

The ESPN announcer on the field asks me, "Is this the greatest day of your life?" My answer is simple. "I haven't had the greatest day of my life yet."

As you can imagine, the locker room is a wild celebration with lots of love going around the room.

When I have finally finished all the media obligations, I am the last one in the coaches' locker room. Cal pokes his head in and says, "Coach, you need anything else?" "No, I'm good, Cal. Thanks for everything. Just tell Cyndy and the girls I'll be out in a minute."

In those final moments before the game, I realized what I wanted. I want to be the man I dreamed about as a kid, not the man I had become. No, it was not worth what I had become to win a championship. But it's never too late to become the person you want to be.

As I walk out of the locker room and see my family, I hug Cyndy and say, "Do you think you can stand me around home more? I just coached my last football game."

With the National Championship trophy in hand, Coach Tim Greene walks away from college football with no remorse.

ABOUT THE AUTHOR

Steve Pederson's professional career includes more than thirty years at the highest levels of college athletics. He began his career as a college football recruiting coordinator assembling No. 1 ranked recruiting classes at The Ohio State University, the University of Tennessee, and the University of Nebraska. From there he spent seventeen years as the Athletic Director at the University of Nebraska and the University of Pittsburgh. During his career, he worked with five Hall of Fame college football coaches and hired the National Basketball Coach of the Year. He lives in Cleveland and New York with his wife, Tami, and their two Golden Retrievers.

Made in the USA
Middletown, DE
30 September 2017